THE GREAT MYSTERY

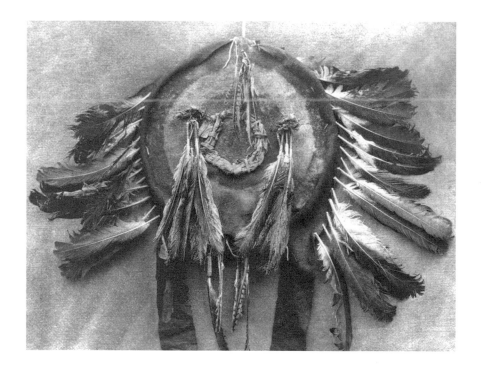

THE GREAT MYSTERY

MYTHS OF NATIVE AMERICA

NEIL PHILIP

CLARION BOOKS
NEW YORK

Clarion Books
a Houghton Mifflin Company imprint
215 Park Avenue South, New York, NY 10003

Published in the United States in 2001 by arrangement with
The Albion Press Ltd, Spring Hill, Idbury, Oxfordshire OX7 6RU, England

The text was set in 13-point Garamond Book.

The extract on p.9 from Joseph Epes Brown, *The Sacred Pipe: Black Elk's Account of the Seven Rites of the Oglala Sioux* copyright © 1953, 1989 by the University of Oklahoma Press, is reproduced courtesy of the University of Oklahoma Press.
For picture sources, see Acknowledgments.

ENDPAPERS: Edward S. Curtis *Looking out of the Painted Cave* Yokuts 1924
HALF-TITLE PAGE: Edward S. Curtis *Shield* Arapaho 1927
TITLE PAGE: Matilde Coxe Stevenson *The Corn Dance* Santa Clara Pueblo 1911
DEDICATION PAGE: Edward S. Curtis *Two Mythical Birds* Kwakiutl 1914
OPPOSITE CONTENTS: Edward S. Curtis *Placating the Spirit of a Slain Eagle* Assiniboin 1926

www.houghtonmifflinbooks.com

Library of Congress Cataloging-in-Publication Data

The great mystery: myths of Native America / [edited by] Neil Philip.
    p. cm.
    Includes bibliographical references and index.
    ISBN 0-395-98405-X
    1. Indian mythology—North America—Juvenile literature. 2. Indians of North America—Religion—Juvenile literature. [1. Indians of North America—Folklore. 2. Folklore—North America.] I. Philip, Neil.
    E98.R3 G72 2001
    398.2'089'97—dc21
                                                                                    2001028289

Printed and bound in Spain on behalf of Midas Printing (UK) Limited,
by Bookprint, S.L., Barcelona.

10 9 8 7 6 5 4 3 2 1

For Emma

CONTENTS

1 A Trail of Beauty   1

2 The Northeast   14

3 The Southeast   29

4 The Plains   43

5 The Southwest   61

6 California   79

7 The Great Basin and Plateau   95

8 The Northwest   111

9 The Arctic   125

Bibliography   136

Acknowledgments   141

Index   142

1 A TRAIL OF BEAUTY

"The Earth was the mother, and the Sky the father." These are the first words of the Maricopa creation myth. While other groups may imagine and express the beginnings of life differently, most Native Americans would agree with the simple truth of these words.

The word "myth" comes from the Greek *mythos*, which means "word" or "story." A myth is a special kind of story—not simply entertainment but a record of sacred events and a basis for ritual and belief. Myths tell us how and why the world came to be, how humankind was created and what our role on earth is, what happens to people when they die, and how the world will end.

Great numbers of myths have been recorded from Native Americans, allowing us privileged access into the mental, emotional, and spiritual world of the tellers. These stories present the secrets of the universe in a kind of narrative poetry.

Like poems, myths have meaning on many levels, and they can be hard to understand. They are often ambiguous, and because they live in spoken—not written—tradition, different versions of the same myth may be contradictory. For example, two characters may be brothers in one version, cousins in a second, father and son in a third.

Although a mythology belongs to a whole people, each particular version of an individual myth belongs to the person who tells it. Myths that are recorded in writing are transmitted through individual tellers, who play a double role. In remembering the story, they are preserving it. And in retelling it, they are making it new. So

Herman Heyn
Last Horse
Sioux 1898

Despite his fierce appearance, with war bonnet, spear, shield, and symbolic war paint on his face and body (including a fearsome "face" on his belly), Last Horse was not on the warpath when this photograph was taken. In fact, he was dressed to impress, ready to take part in sham battles to entertain visitors to the Trans-Mississippi and International Exposition in Omaha. A Sioux warrior sometimes hung an ornament from his ear to signify that he had killed a man, and he had to earn the right to suspend eagle quills from his scalp lock by battle feats. Last Horse's shield shows a Sioux warrior under the protection of Wambli, the eagle, whose spirit is responsible for war parties and battles.

1

the process of handing it on involves both conservation and creation.

At different times, and to different tellers, different aspects of the myth seem more important than others. Myths are not fixed truths but flexible representations of the truth. Therefore, they evolve and change with the times. For instance, when Istet Woiche, a member of the Madesiwi band of the Achomawi tribe of northern California, related his tribe's myths to C. Hart Merriam in the early twentieth century, he included a passage in which the creator, World's Heart, sets the world turning. Istet Woiche was, as Merriam put it, "a remarkably learned man." Having heard that the earth spins on its axis, it is probable that he himself credited this marvel to World's Heart and reasoned that, "If the earth did not travel, there would be no wind." The fact that his grandfather would probably not have recognized this detail does not make Istet Woiche's version of the Madesiwi mythology any less true.

Because myths are able to change in this way, it is impossible to make hard-and-fast statements that hold true for every possible telling or interpretation of any given myth. In this book, which divides Native American mythology into eight loosely defined culture areas, I have tried to bring out the main themes that dominate each area's myths and to illustrate them with specific examples. But while the themes persist, the characters and stories that express these themes often vary. Like the world they describe, they are always transforming themselves.

To take one instance, Taiowa is a Hopi god variously described as the son or brother of the Sun. He is the Hopi equivalent of Paiyatemu, the flute-playing Zuñi sun youth kachina. Taiowa plays a role in various Hopi ceremonies and is revered as the god who taught the

mysteries of the Wuwuchim male initiation rites. But most scholarly accounts downplay his importance; one describes him only as "a minor god of ornaments and wealth." The best reference book on the subject, Sam Gill and Irene Sullivan's *Dictionary of Native American Mythology*, contains no entry for him. The best survey, John Bierhorst's *The Mythology of Native America*, does

not feature him. The best collection, *American Indian Myths and Legends* by Richard Erdoes and Alfonso Ortiz, contains a Hopi creation myth that fails to mention him.

Yet if we turn to the myths that were given by thirty Hopi elders to Frank Waters and published as *The Book of the Hopi*, on the opening page we read, "But first, they say, there was only the Creator, Taiowa. All else was endless space. There was no beginning and no end, no time, no shape, no life. Just an immeasurable void that had its beginning and end, time, shape, and life in the mind of Taiowa the Creator." Telling their myths for a new purpose, the Hopi elders revealed a different facet of their beliefs.

A similar example can be found with the Zuñi. Early myth texts speak of a single creator deity, Awonawilona, who is both male and female, and who brought into being the Earth Mother and Sky Father. Modern commentators say that this creator is *not* a single being, but rather a collection of powerful spirits, known as the Ones Who Hold Our Roads, who are honored in Zuñi prayers and rituals. The Ones Who Hold Our Roads include the Sun Father and Moonlight-Giving Mother. They are what is termed "raw people," as opposed to human beings, who are "cooked people." Raw people are able to transform themselves into any shape they like, whereas cooked people are fixed in their human shape.

Many Native American myths tell of the doings of these "raw people"—the First People, who are both human *and* animal and who shaped the world in the creation time. As one Apache storyteller put it, "They say that all the animals were people in those days." These animal-people are our ancestors and teachers and are still the source of the magical power that the Iroquois call *orenda*. This power is innate in nature and can be harnessed to bring rain or success in the hunt, or for any other purpose, good or bad.

The purpose of many rituals is to petition the spirits for such power, which can also be obtained through dreams or visions. It was to acquire this power that many Native American boys endured the privations of a "vision quest" in the transition to manhood.

Edward S. Curtis
Snake Priest
Hopi 1900

The Snake Dance is a nine-day ceremony for rain and fertility held every other year. This Snake priest is dressed for the penultimate day of the Snake Dance, during which the dance and ceremonial race of the Antelope Society are performed; the white markings on his body represent the antelope. In his right hand he holds his "snake whip"—a pair of eagle feathers used to stroke snakes during the dance to prevent them from coiling and striking. This is necessary because, during the dance, the Snake priests hold live snakes in their mouths. The priests are not bitten because the snakes are their clan brothers. After the dance, the snakes are released unharmed into the wild, to take the prayers of the Hopi to the gods.

Some commentators have spent a great deal of time and energy organizing the spirits of Native American mythologies into hierarchical "pantheons," like those of gods and goddesses of ancient Greece and Rome. For instance, J. R. Walker, a white doctor who worked at the Pine Ridge Reservation from 1896 to 1914, painstakingly assembled an elaborate mythology for the Lakota (the Teton Sioux). Although he did not make anything up, later researchers who tried to verify his myths found that the Lakota themselves were completely baffled by his elaborate versions. Edgar Fire Thunder, a close friend of George Sword, Walker's chief informant, said simply, "Tales never were related in that manner."

The Lakota refer to everything sacred or mysterious as *wakan* and to the power that created and sustains the world as Wakan Tanka, the Great Mystery. As with the Zuñi Awonawilona, Wakan Tanka is sometimes referred to as a single all-seeing deity but should properly be understood as a group of spirits, conventionally said to number sixteen, or "Four Times Four." Little Wound told J. R. Walker, "Wakan Tanka are many. But they are all the same as one."

The ethnologist Francis La Flesche, himself an Omaha, explained how the Mysterious Power of the universe was named Wakon'da. He and his colleague Alice Fletcher defined Wakon'da not as a god but as an unseen, all-pervading life-force.

> An invisible and continuous life was believed to permeate all things, seen and unseen. This life manifests itself in two ways: first, by causing to move—all motion, all acts of mind or body are because of this invisible life; second, by causing permanency of structure and form, as in the rock, the physical features of the landscape, mountains, plains, rivers, lakes, the animals and man. This invisible life was also conceived of as being similar to the will power of which man is

8

conscious within himself—a power by which things are brought to pass. Through this mysterious life and power all things are related to one another and to man, the seen to the unseen, the dead to the living, a fragment of anything to its entirety. This invisible life and power was called Wakon'da.

The whole world is sacred, and everything in it is infused with the living spirit of the Great Mystery. This basic belief lies at the heart of all Native American myths. Black Elk, the famous holy man of the Oglala Sioux, referred to it when describing to Joseph Epes Brown the sweat lodge used in the Lakota rite of purification.

> The willows which make the frame of the sweat lodge are set up in such a way that they mark the four quarters of the universe; thus, the whole lodge is the universe in an image, and the two-legged, four-legged, and winged peoples, and all things of the world, are contained within it, for all these peoples and things, too, must be purified before they can send a voice to Wakan Tanka.
>
> The rocks which we use represent Grandmother Earth, from whom all fruits come, and they also represent the indestructible and everlasting nature of Wakan Tanka. The fire which is used to heat the rocks represents the great power of Wakan Tanka which gives life to all things; it is as a ray from the sun, for the sun is also Wakan Tanka in a certain aspect.
>
> The round fireplace at the center of the sweat lodge is the center of the universe, in which dwells Wakan Tanka, with His power which is the fire. All these things are *wakan* to us and must be understood deeply if we really wish to purify ourselves, for the power of a thing or an act is in the meaning and the understanding.

This kind of representation of the universe in miniature is central to many Native American rituals. The number four, which represents completeness in so

Francis La Flesche
Bacon Rind
Osage 1900

This Osage chief—an initiate into the Bear Clan priesthood—is tattooed with the mark of honor, a symbolic prayer for long life and fertility. The design represents a stone knife, tents, and two pipes. The meaning of the design is "The sacred pipe has descended." The tattooing was a ritual that marked entry into adulthood and bound the warrior to faithfully keep the rites of the pipe. A warrior who had cut off the heads of enemies in battle could have skulls tattooed at the ends of the three bands that appear over each shoulder, thus drawing to himself the strength of those he had killed. The design of the tattoo is slightly obscured by a handsome shell gorget at Bacon Rind's throat and an 1857 James Buchanan Peace Medal hanging from his neck.

many myths and tales, reminds us of the importance of the four cardinal directions—north, south, east, west—in Native American thought. In addition to these four directions, which give us our bearings on the earth, there are two others equally important—up (to the sky world) and down (to the world below). And anchoring all six of these directions is the most important of all—the center.

The elaborate Buffalo Dance of the Mandan, which was called the Okeepa, incorporated in almost every aspect of its rituals the Mandan's belief that they lived at the very center of the world.

The Okeepa was partly an initiation ceremony in which young men entered manhood with sacrifices to the Great Spirit. It was partly a dramatic re-creation of the founding myths of Mandan culture. It was partly a kind of magical rite to ensure a plentiful supply of buffalo to hunt in the coming season. And it was, above all, a ritual of world renewal. The Mandan believed that if the Okeepa were not performed, a new flood would rise to destroy the world, as it had once before in the dawn of time.

The Mandan myths incorporate many themes that crop up again and again in Native American mythology: the creation of the world from mud brought up from the bottom of the primeval ocean by an "earth diver"—in this case, a mudhen; the shaping of the earth by twin creators, First Creator and Lone Man; the transformation of First Creator into Coyote, the trickster, while Lone Man, the culture hero, teaches the people how to live; the emergence of the Mandan (whose name for themselves, Numakaki, simply means "the people") from beneath the earth; the great flood that both destroys and renews the world.

The era in which most Native American myths are

set—what I call the creation time—is not located in the past but in the present, an eternal present that is constantly renewing itself. In ritual, in prayer, in song, dance, drama, and storytelling, human beings can enter that eternal present, a world that is outside time as defined by clocks and calendars. While clock time proceeds onward in a straight line, like a walk from one place to another, myth time works in circles, like the cycle of the year, always coming back to the point where it started. An example from Native American mythology is Changing Woman, the chief Navajo goddess, who grows old and then young again with the seasons.

In such ceremonies as the Mandan Okeepa, the winter dances of the Bella Coola, the ritual cycle of the Hopi, and the first-fruits festival of the Creek, the enactment of mythical scenes—usually by masked dancers impersonating spirits—enables the people to interact with the spirit world. By confirming the compact between the seen and the unseen, the balance of life is maintained and the world is renewed.

The ethnologist George Bird Grinnell records in his book *Pawnee Hero Stories and Folk-Tales* what he was told of the secret rites of the Pawnee medicine lodge by Major Frank North, the white commander of the Pawnee Scouts. North watched a Pawnee medicine man break up a piece of the hard earth floor of the lodge, moisten it, plant a few kernels of corn, and then sing the corn into growth before his eyes. When the plant ripened, the medicine man plucked a new ear of corn and passed it among the watchers. In ancient Greece, the priests who celebrated the famous Mysteries of Eleusis demonstrated the promise of new life after death in the same way, by displaying an ear of corn. And they did it for the same purpose—to "hold the human race together."

The seriousness with which Native Americans took their sacred trust to keep the world going can be seen in the passage from Black Elk quoted above, or in the warning issued to all those initiated into the Winnebago medicine rite. "Never tell anyone about this rite," they were instructed. "Keep it absolutely secret. If you disclose it, the world will come to an end. We will all die."

When it seemed as if the only way to preserve the rite was to disclose it, a Winnebago named Jasper Blowsnake did tell its secrets to the ethnologist Paul Radin. The title of Radin's book about the rite, *The Road of Life and Death*, names the sacred road that all traditional Native Americans walk.

In the chapters that follow, you may walk with them, part of the way—"wandering along a trail of beauty," in the words of the Navajo Nightway chant.

Edward S. Curtis
Two Whistles
Crow 1908

Two Whistles, a Mountain Crow of the Not Mixed Clan, was born in 1856. A noted warrior, he first fasted for a vision at the age of thirty-five, wailing, "He That Hears Always, hear my cries. As my tears drop to the ground, look upon me." The first night he saw the war bonnet of a Sioux. The next day he cut the skin and flesh of his arms in the pattern of eight hoofprints, and that night the Moon came to him and told him where to find buffalo and horses, saying, "You will never be poor." The hawk fixed to his hair is his medicine, or spirit helper, which he purchased from a Sioux with a horse. After purchasing a medicine, the buyer must still fast for a vision to know whether he has been accepted.

2 THE NORTHEAST

The peoples of the Northeast, such as the Iroquois and the Algonquin, were the first to have their myths, legends, and customs recorded. Their ideas have therefore greatly influenced the way people think about Native American mythology.

The Iroquois, known as "the people of the longhouse," lived by fishing and agriculture in fortified villages. Very early on (most histories say 1570, but it may well have been even earlier) they founded the Confederacy of the League of the Iroquois. This bound together five great nations—the Seneca, Cayuga, Onondaga, Oneida, and Mohawk; a sixth, the Tuscarora, was accepted into the confederacy in 1715. Their unity was crucial when they had to respond to the gradual encroachment of white settlers on their traditional lands in the lowlands of the Lawrence River.

The Iroquois creation story is perhaps the best known of all Native American myths: the one that has given North America the name by which many Native Americans know it—Turtle Island. It is found in various versions, but the basic outline is always the same. What follows is a Seneca version.

> Beyond the sky there is another world, and the great chief of this sky world was called the Ancient One. In the center of the sky world there grew a great tree whose flowers and fruit sustained all the people who lived there.
>
> Now, the Ancient One took Old Woman to be his wife. But this marriage did not make the Ancient One happy. He began to waste away, and his bones became dry and brittle.

He fell into a deep and troubled sleep and dreamed that the answer to his problems was to uproot the tree. So the Ancient One summoned all his strength, clasped his arms around the tree, and pulled it out by the roots, leaving a great hole in the floor of the sky world.

Then he called Old Woman to look through the hole, and when she came, he pushed her through it. As she fell, she grabbed seeds from the tree with one hand, and a tobacco-scented root with the other.

In those days there were no human beings on the earth, and the whole world was covered in water. The ducks on the water saw Old Woman fall and decided to save her. So they wove their wings together, and caught her.

Then the Great Turtle rose from the underworld and with the curve of his shell made a resting place for her above the water.

The ducks and other water creatures began to dive down below the surface, searching for soil to set on the turtle's back to make it more comfortable. They all tried, but none could dive far enough. Then, at last, the muskrat managed to just touch his nose upon the bottom and bring up some mud. He smeared this earth on the turtle's shell, and at once it began to grow and spread, and the turtle grew with it.

All this time Old Woman was lying unconscious. But now she stirred and released from her hands the seeds she had plucked from the sky tree. From them all kinds of plants began to grow. And from the root sprang up a new tree, just like the marvelous one in the sky.

Old Woman built herself a lodge beneath this tree, and in the course of time she gave birth to a daughter, who soon grew to be a young woman. Old Woman sent this daughter out every day to explore the island. The Wind took a liking to her, embraced her, and made her pregnant.

Soon she heard two voices inside her arguing as to which would be born first. One voice was kind and gentle, but the other was harsh and rough. This second voice said, "I shall push my way out through our

mother's armpit." And that is what he did, in order to be born first. The mother had just enough strength to give birth to her second child in the normal way, and then she died.

She was the first being to die and to make a path from this world back to the sky world. From her grave grew corn, beans, and squash, the three sisters who are the supporters of life, and tobacco, whose smoke rises as incense to the sky.

Her firstborn was named Flint, because his heart was made of flint, and the second was called Sky

Holder. Their grandmother, Old Woman, welcomed Sky Holder and looked after him, but she threw Flint away, into a hollow tree.

As Sky Holder grew, he began to go out every morning to hunt, but every night he came home without his bow and arrows. When he was asked what he had done with them, he said, "I gave them to the boy in the hollow tree." So Old Woman relented, and they fetched Flint home, and she brought the two boys up together.

When they were fully grown, the twin boys decided to enlarge the island. Flint went west and created the hill country, all rocks and ledges, while Sky Holder went east and created a land of streams and meadows. Flint was angry when he saw the land Sky Holder had made. "You are making it too easy," he said, and he did everything he could to spoil the new land. While Sky Holder made all the useful animals and plants, Flint followed behind him making the poisonous ones. Once Flint even stole the sun and hid it in the southwest, and even though Sky Holder won it back, Flint had invented winter.

Gazing into a pool, Sky Holder saw his own reflection and decided to make human beings in his image. He molded six pairs of them out of clay—the first man and the first woman of each of the Six Nations of the Iroquois—and gave each of them a place of their own and taught them how to live. But Flint matched Sky Holder's good gifts with bad ones, bringing disease and evil into the world.

At last Sky Holder and Flint fought, and Sky Holder vanquished his brother and imprisoned him in a cave.

When his work was done, Sky Holder followed his mother's path up to the world in the sky.

This myth contains many themes that are repeated in stories told throughout the Northeast, among the Algonquin as well as the Iroquois. Eagentci, Old Woman, is also known as First Mother.

In Penobscot mythology, First Mother sacrifices herself to save the early humans from starvation, and corn and

Edward S. Curtis
A Chipewyan Tipi Among the Aspens
Chipewyan 1926

The subarctic Chipewyan are known as "the dog-ribbed people" because the first female, Copper Woman, was married to a dog who turned into a man at night. The Chipewyan and other Athapaskan peoples are their descendants. The Chipewyan believe that power and knowledge can be gained in dreams and used either positively in healing or hunting or negatively in sorcery. They call this Power inkoze; the Seneca call it orenda. According to the Menomini, "Power is white, like the sun when it is shining."

tobacco grow from her flesh and bones. She dies so that "her power should be felt over the whole world and that all men should love her." Old Woman is, to all intents and purposes, the earth—one of her Seneca names translates as Mature Flower or Fertile Earth.

The role of the muskrat in bringing up the first mud from the bottom of the primeval ocean is echoed by earth divers in many Native American cultures, where animals as diverse as the beaver, the mink, and the loon are credited with this vital act of creation.

Sky Holder and Flint have parallels in many stories in which the earth is co-created by two brothers, one of whom makes life easy for mankind, the other of whom makes it difficult. The North Atlantic Coast duo are Glooscap and his wolf twin brother, Malsum, whose exploits were celebrated by tribes such as the Micmac and Passamaquoddy; among the Lenape, they are Welsit Manatu (the Good Spirit) and Mahtantu (the Evil Spirit).

Sky Holder's retreat into the sky after his work of creation is done is also typical. Some say that Sky Holder, wishing to teach mankind how to be happy, chose to be born again as a mortal—in the shape of Hiawatha, a young man of the Onondaga nation. The name Hiawatha, meaning "he who makes rivers," is certainly a suitable name for Sky Holder in human shape.

The next story is the tale of Hiawatha as told by Chief Big Kittle of the Seneca in 1905; other versions give the role of lawmaker to Deganawida, but in any case Hiawatha and Deganawida are so alike as to be essentially twin aspects of the same person.

> Where the Mohawk River empties into the Hudson, there was once a Mohawk village whose people were fierce and warlike, and lived only to take the scalps of their enemies.
>
> Among the Mohawk was a chief named Deganawida,

a wise man who loved peace. But when he spoke in
council and pleaded with the young warriors to stop
killing, they laughed at him. So, weeping, Deganawida
left his people and journeyed west.

Sitting and meditating by a lake, Deganawida heard
the sound of a man skillfully paddling a canoe. He
looked out and saw a man lean from his canoe, dip a
basket into the water, and bring it up full of shells.

Then the man paddled his canoe to the shore, got
out, lit a fire, and began to string the shells. For a long
time Deganawida watched secretly as the man made
shell strings in the firelight.

At last curiosity overcame him, and he stepped out
onto the sand, saying, "I am a friend! I am Deganawida
of the Mohawk."

And the man replied, "I am Hiawatha of the
Onondaga."

"What are those strings you are making?" asked
Deganawida.

"They are the rules of life and the laws of good gov-
ernment," said Hiawatha. "This string of white shells is
a symbol of truth, peace, and goodwill. This string of
black shells is a symbol of hate, war, and bad faith.
This string of alternating black and white beads is a
symbol that peace should exist between nations. And
this string with white on either end and black in the
middle is a sign that all war must end."

"You are my friend," said Deganawida, "and the friend of all men. War makes us weak, not strong."

"I agree," said Hiawatha. "But Atotarho, chief of the Onondaga, would not listen to me. He slew my brothers and drove me away."

"Come with me," said Deganawida, "and we shall tell my people of your new rules and laws."

So they went to the Mohawk, and then to the Oneida, and then to the Cayuga, and convinced them all to leave off war and take up peace.

Then they went and tried to speak to Atotarho about this new way of life. But Atotarho was so angry that he could not speak. He ran mad into the forest, where he gnawed at his fingers and ate grass and leaves. His evil thoughts sprouted from his skull like serpents, waving in a tangled mass and hissing venom.

But Deganawida did not fear him and kept speaking to him about peace and friendship while Hiawatha combed the snakes from his hair. Deganawida told Atotarho that if he wished he should be the head chief of the confederacy and govern it according to the new laws that Hiawatha had made.

When Atotarho at last had calmed down, he accepted their offer, saying, "We should ask the Seneca to join us, too. Otherwise, they will be jealous and will eat us all."

So the Seneca joined, and the five nations made a peace pact and built the first longhouse. Deganawida was its builder, and Hiawatha was its designer.

The shell beads Hiawatha strung by the lake are called wampum, and wampum belts that record agreements and treaties are still held as sacred by the Iroquois.

The world tree of the Seneca was said to have branches that pierced the sky and roots that delved down into the underworld. Hawenniyo, the Great Protector and chief of the False Faces of the Iroquois (a medicine society whose members dance in ritual masks), represents the creator. He is the guardian of the world tree, and the False Faces rub their turtle-shell rattles on pine trees to obtain power.

Anonymous
Six Chiefs of the Iroquois
Iroquois 1871

These Iroquois chiefs, photographed on the Six Nations Reserve, Ontario, Canada, are holding wampum belts that record the history of agreements and treaties both among the members of the Six Nations and with other tribes and with whites. The deep symbolism of wampum strings and belts is enshrined in the myth of Hiawatha and Deganawida. The shell beads known as wampum were used for trade and decoration as well as for tribal records, but wampum is not simply a form of money. It has a profound spiritual importance. Wampum was believed to be created by shamans smoking the sacred pipe—an act of reverence to the Great Spirit. They sucked in smoke and spat out wampum.

The Wampum Code of the Five Nations Confederacy refers to Deganawida uprooting "the tallest pine tree," so that the chiefs may cast their weapons of war into the cavity, and then replanting the tree, now known as the Tree of the Long Leaves or the Tree of Peace. It is under this tree that the nations shelter, and there is an eagle at its peak to warn of the approach of enemies.

The longhouse—once the home of a whole village, now the council chamber—remains the symbol of Iroquois unity. Among the Seneca it is also the focus of the belief system known as the "longhouse religion," founded by the prophet Handsome Lake in 1799 to preserve their traditional way of life.

Another visionary with a message that was similar to Handsome Lake's was the Shawnee prophet Tenskatawa, brother of the great leader Tecumseh. Tenskatawa brought a message of renewed cultural vitality directly from the Great Spirit, and his teachings provided the spiritual background to his brother's dream of uniting all the Native American nations from Canada to the Gulf of Mexico to defend their land and culture from the whites.

Algonquian-speaking tribes around the Great Lakes—such as the Ojibwe, Menomini, and Shawnee—saw Tenskatawa (whose name means "the open door") not simply as a prophet or medicine man, but as the incarnation of the god Winabojo, who is essentially the central Algonquian equivalent of Sky Holder.

He is the powerful god who brought the animals and plants into being. His name is spelled in all kinds of ways (Winabojo, Manobozho, Menapus, Nanabush), but it always means "Big Rabbit." However, unlike other creator-trickster gods of Native America, he is always thought of in human form.

In one of Winabojo's escapades, he tries to hook the king of the fishes with his line but instead is swallowed up—line, canoe, and all. The fish king is no happier about it than he is, saying, "I feel sick for having swallowed this dirty fellow Winabojo."

With the help of a squirrel, Winabojo manages to wedge the fish king's throat open with his canoe, but he still can't get out. At last he kills the fish by attacking its

A. E. Jenks
A Medicine Man and Dancers Within the Midewiwin
Ojibwe 1899

The Midewiwin, or grand medicine lodge, is the center of Ojibwe ritual life. Each initiate is "shot" with small shells, "dies," and is revived by the Mide priest, who sucks the shells from his body. The initiates rise through eight levels of training, each with its own healing songs and secret knowledge. The Midewiwin was originated by Shell-Covered One, who sent Bear to the creator to ask for help to counteract disease and death. The helping spirits gave Bear the "pack of life," a medicine bundle. This is reflected in Mide lore: each level has its own sacred medicine bag, containing sacred white shells from which the songs call forth help in healing.

heart and, when it comes to shore, Winabojo is rescued by the gulls.

One Menomini story tells how Winabojo got into trouble watching a ball game—the traditional Native American sport now known as lacrosse.

It happened that the beings of the world above challenged the beings of the world below to a ball game. One goal was at Detroit and the other was at Chicago, with the center at a spot near Sturgeon Bay on Lake Michigan.

The beings above called on the thunderbirds, the eagles, the geese, the ducks, the pigeons, and all the birds of the air to play for them, while the great white bear called upon the fishes, the snakes, the otters, the deer, and all the beasts of the field to play for the powers below.

The game was about to start when Winabojo happened along. Nobody had told him anything about it. When he learned what was going on, he said, "I must see this, even though I wasn't invited."

When the chiefs of the underworld gathered high up on a mountaintop from which they could survey the whole field, Winabojo was with them, disguised as a tall pine tree, burned on one side.

At dawn he heard a great hubbub and whooping. From every direction he heard voices calling "Hau! Hau! Hau!" and "Hoo! Hoo! Hoo!" to taunt the enemy.

The birds and the beasts arrived on the field, silence fell, and the players lined up, the weakest nearest the goals and the strongest in the center. Someone tossed the ball high into the air, and the game commenced. The howling and whooping were deafening. The players surged back and forth, now this side and now that gaining the advantage.

At last the ball was carried to the Chicago goal. The activity was so violent that all Winabojo could see was a cloud of dust. Straining to see what was going on, he forgot where he was and changed from a tree back into a man.

Winabojo was in a tight spot, but he had the advantage of surprise. He quickly drew his bow and shot two arrows at each of the underworld gods. Alarmed, the underworld gods rushed down the mountain to take refuge in the water. They made such a splash as they dived into the lake that they sent great waves rolling across the treetops toward the Chicago goal.

The game had to be abandoned. The angry players soon realized that it had been Winabojo's doing. "Nobody else would dare to attack the underworld gods." So they decided to hunt him down and make him pay. "We will use the power of water for our guide," they said.

They asked the water to find Winabojo for them, and it pursued him. However fast Winabojo ran, when he looked back, there was the water flowing after him. He ran faster and faster, but still it came.

Winabojo began to get very worried. On and on he fled, but the water kept gaining.

James Mooney
The Dance Before the Ball Game
Cherokee 1888

The ball game, from which modern lacrosse derives, was not just a sport but a serious part of ritual life. Among southeastern peoples such as the Cherokee and the Creek, play could turn quite violent, and the game was sometimes called "the younger brother of war." The Cherokee used the phrase "play a ball game" to mean "fight a battle." Ritual dances beforehand emphasized the spiritual aspect of the game. Here, seven women dancers line up behind the lacrosse sticks; their dance leader sits in front of them, ready to strike a rhythm for them on a drum. The seven male players circle counterclockwise around a fire to the accompaniment of their dance leader shaking a gourd rattle. Two or three days before the game, the players were scratched on the chest and arm with a seven-toothed turkey-bone comb. The Cherokee, Creeks, and Seminoles all tell myths of the ball game between the birds and the animals.

This Ojibwe man is mending his birch-bark canoe by patching the seams with tree gum. As canoes were a chief mode of transport through the intricate waterways of the Northeast, they naturally feature in several myths. For instance, Winabojo has a magic canoe that will go wherever he tells it to. In a Passamaquoddy story, Joseph, the youngest of three brothers, helps an old woman and is rewarded first with a pair of wooden moccasins that enable him to run faster than the swiftest animal, then with a dugout canoe that can soar across the water, and finally with a canoe that can fly through the air. He flies away, leaving his jealous brothers gasping in astonishment, and journeys over strange lands and seas before at last returning home.

At last he came to a high mountain, on the top of which grew a lofty pine.

"I'll go up there and ask for help," thought Winabojo.

He raced up the mountainside, with the water rising swiftly behind him. "My dear little brother," gasped Winabojo to the pine tree, "help me!"

"How?" asked the pine.

"Let me climb up you, and every time I reach the top, grow another length," said Winabojo.

"I haven't so much power as all that," said the pine. "I can only grow four lengths."

"That will do, I'll take it!" screamed the terrified Winabojo, jumping into the branches just ahead of the water. He climbed as fast as he could, but the water began to wet his feet as it rose behind him. Soon Winabojo was at the top of the tree. "Little brother, stretch yourself," he begged.

The tree grew one length, Winabojo climbed higher, and the water followed. Twice more he begged the pine to stretch itself, and each time it grew another length.

At last Winabojo prayed, "Stretch yourself just once more, little brother—just one more length. Maybe that will save me. If it doesn't, I shall be drowned." Up shot the pine tree for the fourth and last time.

Winabojo climbed to the top, and still the water followed—but it stopped just where it touched his feet, and did not rise any farther. So Winabojo was stuck there, frightened half to death, clinging to the top of the tall pine tree.

This is a good place for us to leave him—stuck in a silly predicament caused by his own mischief-making. It is typical of the stories about him.

The Menomini see the world as an island, floating in a limitless ocean and separating the universe into upper and lower layers. In the upper layer are the benevolent powers, such as the sun, the stars, and the thunderbirds, and in the lower layer are the malevolent powers, such as the Great White Bear, with a long copper tail, who

holds up the earth as the Great Spirit holds up the sky, and the horned serpents that are the special enemies of the thunderbirds. The Menomini themselves get supernatural power from the spirits by fasting, dreaming, and dancing in the ritual Medicine Dance and Dream Dance.

The Native Americans of the Northeast recognized a supreme deity, known to the Ojibwe as Gichi Manitou, which means the Great Spirit or the Great Mystery. The word "*manitou*" (in various spellings) is also used for the lesser spirits, both good and bad, that inhabit all of nature—animals, trees, rocks, and such powerful forces as wind and thunder.

These lesser *manitous* tend to dominate both myths and rituals, leaving Gichi Manitou as a rather remote deity, not sharply differentiated from other important divinities such as the Master of Life, who is in charge of all souls, both human and animal, or the Sky Holder. As a result, when Christianity was preached to them, the northeastern nations tended to adapt their existing gods

Anonymous
*Ojibwe and
Menomini Drummers
and Dancers*
Ojibwe and
Menomini c. 1910

*The Medicine Dance
and Dream Dance of the
Menomini are rituals to
obtain power from the
spirits. The rituals of the
Menomini medicine
lodge involve a
dramatization of the
story of Menapus, or Big
Rabbit. The novice acts
the part of Menapus,
while the medicine men
leading the ritual
impersonate the Great
Gods Below and Above.
The first drum was
given to a young
woman who lay hidden
from the whites for eight
days; she was rescued
by the Great Spirit, who
told her, "When you feel
sad at heart, or sick, or
fear war, or desire
victory in battle, tell it
to the drum, which you
shall call your
grandfather, and give it
a present of tobacco,
and your words shall be
wafted to me."*

to suit the new framework. Among the Seneca, for instance, Hawenniyo, the master of the False Faces, came to be identified with the Christian God, while Flint was identified with the Devil; but Sky Holder remains as the focus of traditional religious belief.

How such thinking worked is illustrated by a Menomini account of the birth of Menapus (Winabojo), given to Alanson Skinner in 1915.

> In the beginning, the Supreme God created the world by putting islands into the great waters. Then he took up some earth like wax and molded in his hand the image of a human being. Then he blew his breath four times upon it, and it came to life and it was his son, Jesus. He placed him across the great waters and gave the land there to him to protect and rule. Then the Supreme God took up red clay, made a tiny image and blew his breath upon it four times. The last time he blew life into the clay and made Menapus, his servant, to protect this island and his grandmother's people, and he decreed that Jesus and Menapus should be friends and brothers, each to remain on his separate island and take care of his people. All went well until Columbus crossed the ocean. . . . Then everything began to conflict, so that now no one in this world can ever understand it.

3 THE SOUTHEAST

The most prominent peoples of the Southeast were the so-called Five Civilized Tribes: the Cherokee, Choctaw, Chickasaw, Creek, and Seminole nations. The largest of these nations, the Cherokee, spoke an Iroquoian language; the others spoke Muskogean languages, related to the language of the Muskogee, the chief tribe of the Creek Confederacy.

There are two basic variants of the creation myth in the Southeast. Peoples such as the Alabama, Creek, and Choctaw say that the first human beings came to the earth from a world below, where they lived in the dark and saw no sun. This is the myth of the emergence, which reaches its most sophisticated form in the Southwest. Other peoples tell creation stories that are more closely related to those of the Northeast, in which the land is created on a primeval sea by the act of an earth diver fetching mud from the bottom. Among the Yuchi the earth diver is a crawfish; among the Cherokee it is a water beetle, Beaver's Grandchild. This is the Cherokee version.

> The earth is a great island floating in a sea of water, and it is suspended at the north, south, east, and west by cords hanging down from the vault of the sky, which is made of solid rock crystal. When the world grows old and worn out, the cords will break and the earth will sink down into the ocean, and all will be water again.
>
> At the beginning, when all was still water, the animals were living in the world above, but it was too crowded. At last Water Beetle offered to go and see what was below. He dived beneath the surface and brought up some soft mud from the bottom, which

James Mooney
A Log Cabin
Cherokee **1888**

This cabin was the home of the medicine man Swimmer, whose mind "was a storehouse of Indian tradition." He can be seen standing behind the woman grinding corn. A Cherokee myth, probably recorded from Swimmer, tells how once some Cherokees noticed that the corn they put into their corn mill was disappearing overnight. The only clue was the tracks of a dog on the ground. The next night they kept watch and saw a dog come from the north and eat the meal. They sprang out, whipping at him, and he ran off howling to his home in the northern sky, with meal dropping from his mouth as he ran. It left a white trail behind him, where now we see the Milky Way, which the Cherokee to this day call "Where the dog ran."

grew to become the earth and was then attached to the sky by the four cords.

The animals sent Buzzard down to make the earth ready for them, but it was still very wet. When he reached the Cherokee country, Buzzard was so tired he found it hard to keep himself up in the air. As his wings flapped they hit the ground, and wherever they struck the earth there was a valley, and where they turned up again there was a mountain. When the animals saw what was happening, they were afraid that the whole world would be mountains, so they called Buzzard back. But the Cherokee country remains full of mountains to this day.

The most important sacred element in the Southeast was fire, the symbol of the sun. At the annual Creek first-fruits festival, all fires were extinguished and a new sacred fire was ritually lit. All fires for the next year were lit from this sacred fire. Two groups of people with close links of trust and friendship were said to be "of one fire."

The sun was vitally important in the mythologies of the southeastern cultures. The society of the Natchez was a hierarchy, with a primary chief called the Great Sun at the top. For some peoples, the sun was female, not male. The Tunica, for instance, danced the Sun Dance in honor of a girl who became the sun. As she went up into the sky, she sang and danced and radiated light all around her. The Yuchi called themselves "the children of the sun"—she was their mother, and they sprang from a drop of her blood that fell to the earth when she first rose to the sky.

One of the most interesting sun myths is the Cherokee tale of the Daughter of the Sun.

> The Sun lived on the other side of the sky vault, but her daughter lived in the middle of the sky. Every day, as she climbed along the sky arch from east to west, the Sun would stop at her daughter's house for her midday meal.

Now, the people of the earth could never look straight at the sun without screwing up their faces. The Sun told her brother, the Moon, "My grandchildren are ugly." But the Moon said, "No, they are handsome," because the people always smiled when they saw his gentle light.

When she learned that everyone smiled at the Moon but frowned at her, the Sun was jealous. She decided to kill all the people. Every day when she got to her daughter's house she sent out stronger and stronger rays, until she caused a great fever.

So many died that soon the people began to fear that no one would be left. They went for help to the Little People, the spirits who live in the rock caves on mountainsides, and the Little People told them that the only way to save themselves was to kill the Sun.

The Little Men changed two men into snakes, the Spreading Adder and the Copperhead. That night they hid by the door of the Daughter of the Sun, ready to bite the Sun when she came the next day. But when the Sun arrived, her light was so blinding that the

Spreading Adder could only spit out yellow slime, which he still does to this day when he tries to bite. And the Copperhead just crawled off without trying to do anything.

The next day the Little Men changed one man into the Uktena, the great horned snake, and another into the Rattlesnake, and sent them to wait once again outside the house of the Daughter of the Sun.

Everyone thought the Uktena was sure to succeed, because he was so large and fearsome. But the Rattlesnake was so quick and eager that he slipped ahead and coiled up alone outside the house. And when the Daughter of the Sun opened the door to look for her mother, the Rattlesnake darted up and bit her. Then he went home, forgetting all about waiting for the Sun.

The Uktena was so angry that he too returned to earth. He is a great snake, as large as a tree trunk, with horns on his head and a crystal like a bright, blazing star on his forehead. He has scales that glitter like sparks of fire, and spots of color along his body. He can only be killed by being shot in the seventh spot from the head, because under this are his heart and his life. Whoever can win a crystal from the head of an Uktena will be a great wonderworker, but only one man has ever done so. The blood of the Uktena is poisonous, and if the Uktena even looks at a man, that man's family will die.

The people did not know what to do with the Uktena. He was too fierce to kill. So they banished him to the underworld with all the other dangerous things.

Now, when the Sun found her daughter dead, she was filled with grief. She locked herself in her daughter's house and would not come out. The people stopped dying from the heat, but the world went dark and cold.

The people went once more to the Little People, who told them that they must journey to the Darkening Land in the west and bring back the Sun's daughter from the Ghost Country. Seven men said they would go, and the Little People gave them a box and seven sourwood rods. The Little People said that when the men got to the Ghost Country, they would find all the ghosts at a dance. They must stand outside the circle, and when the Sun's daughter danced past them, they must strike her with the rods. She would fall to the ground, and they must put her in the box and take her to her mother. But they must not open the box, even a little way, until they were home again.

The seven men traveled for seven days to the west until they came to the Darkening Land. All the people there were having a dance, just as if they were back

James Mooney
Swimmer
Cherokee **1888**

Swimmer (Ayuñini) is shown holding his gourd rattle, the badge of his authority as a principal medicine man of the Cherokee. It was from Swimmer that the ethnologist James Mooney recorded the bulk of Cherokee mythology, and the medicine man also entrusted Mooney with a manuscript of sacred formulas and songs written in the Cherokee alphabet devised by Sequoyah. Swimmer was born about 1835. When he died in 1899, he "was buried like a true Cherokee on the slope of a forest-clad mountain. Peace to his ashes and sorrow for his going, for with him perished half the tradition of a people."

home. The Sun's daughter was in the outer circle. When all seven men had touched her with their rods, she fell out of the ring, and they put her in the box and closed the lid fast. The other ghosts did not seem to notice what had happened.

The men took the box and started home toward the east. In a little while the girl came back to life and begged to be let out of the box, but they ignored her pleas. Soon she called again, saying she was hungry, but still they made no answer. After another while she begged them for a drink, but the men carrying the box said nothing and still went on.

When at last they were very near home, she called again, begging them to raise the lid just a little. "I can't breathe in here," she said.

They were afraid she would die, so they lifted the lid a crack to give her air. As they did so, there was a fluttering sound inside, and something flew past them into the thicket. They heard a redbird cry, *Kwish! Kwish! Kwish!* in the bushes.

They shut down the lid fast and went on again to the settlements. But when they got there and opened the box, it was empty.

So we know the Redbird is the Daughter of the Sun. If the men had kept the box closed, as the Little People told them to, they would have brought her home safely, and we could bring back our other friends from the Ghost Country. But now when they die, we can never bring them back.

The Sun was glad when the men set out for the Ghost Country, but when they came back without her daughter, her grief broke out even more violently than before. "My daughter! My daughter!" she cried, and she wept until her tears made a flood upon the earth, and the people were afraid they would be drowned.

They sent all the most handsome young men and women to try to make her stop crying. They danced for her and sang her all their best songs, but for a long time the Sun kept her face covered and would not look or listen.

Then the drummer changed the rhythm and started to play a funny song, and despite herself, the Sun began to laugh. She uncovered her face, and the world was filled with light.

And since then, the Sun has never shone so fiercely as to cause people to die; but they still cannot look at her without squinting.

This myth is particularly interesting because the grand elements are so beautifully balanced with simple human emotions. Here, as in life, when jealousy, anger, and grief threaten the world, only laughter can renew it.

Myths told right across North America feature the Orpheus motif, in which someone tries and just barely fails to rescue a loved one from the land of the dead, thus sealing death as permanent and irreversible.

The idea of changing men into snakes, or a girl into a bird, is not suprising to a Native American, to whom there is no inherent difference between man and animal. As the Caddo, another southeastern tribe, put it, "The people and the animals all lived together and were the same in the beginning of the world." The animals are regarded as living much as humans do, with their own chiefs and townhouses, councils and ball games, and they go to the same hereafter in the Darkening Land. Thus, hunters who kill animals must ask their pardon.

Just as gods such as Rabbit the trickster—a common hero of the southeastern myths—can take both human and animal form, so, too, can medicine men transform themselves into animals. One Cherokee medicine man, for instance, turned himself into a hummingbird in order to steal tobacco for mankind.

Bears were originally a human clan of the Cherokee. How they became bears is told in the following tale.

Long ago there was a Cherokee clan called the Ani-Tsaguhi, and in one family of this clan was a boy who used to love to wander in the mountains. After a while, he went oftener and stayed longer, until at last

Anonymous
Pounding Corn
Choctaw c. 1900

Corn was the gift of Corn Woman and was pounded into meal in mortars usually made from hickory logs. One Caddo myth tells how the greedy trickster Coyote turned himself into such a corn mill so that he could eat all the corn himself. The women grinding the corn wondered where it was all going, and one of them fetched an ax to split the log open. As she raised the ax, Coyote rolled away and, turning back into himself, made his escape.

he would not eat in the house at all but started off at daybreak and did not come back until night. His parents scolded him, but that did no good. He still stayed out all day.

After a while, his parents noticed that long brown hair was beginning to sprout all over his body. They wondered at this and asked him, "What do you do all day? Why will you never eat at home?"

"I find plenty to eat in the woods," the boy replied. "And I like it better than the corn and beans we have in the settlements. Pretty soon I am going into the woods to stay all the time."

His parents were worried by this and begged him not to leave them, but he said, "It is better there than here. You can see that I am beginning to change already. I will not be able to live here any longer. Why not come with me? There is plenty for all of us, and you will never have to work for it. But if you want to come, you must first fast for seven days."

His father and mother talked it over, and then consulted the headmen of the clan. They held a council about the matter, and after everything had been said, the clan decided, "Here we work hard, yet still there is not enough. In the woods, he says there is always plenty, and you never have to work. We will go with him." So they fasted for seven days, and on the seventh morning all the Ani-Tsaguhi left the settlement and started for the mountains, with the boy leading the way.

When the other clans heard about it, they were very sad, and they sent their headmen to persuade the Ani-Tsaguhi to stay at home and not go into the woods to live. The messengers found the Ani-Tsaguhi already on the way and were amazed to see that they had started sprouting hair like animals. For seven days they had not taken human food, and now their nature was changing.

But the Ani-Tsaguhi would not come back. They said, "We are going where there is always plenty to eat. From now on we shall be called *yanu*, bears. When you are hungry, come into the woods and we shall give you our own flesh to eat. You need not be afraid

to kill us, for we shall live forever." Then they taught
the messengers the songs with which to call them, and
the bear hunters use those songs still.

   When they had finished, the Ani-Tsaguhi went on
their way, and the messengers turned back toward the
settlements. After a little while, they looked back and
saw no people, only a drove of bears shambling into
the woods.

James Mooney collected two of the "simple and plain-
tive" songs that the Ani-Tsaguhi taught the messengers.
The bear hunter must start out each morning fasting and
not eat until evening. As he leaves camp, he must sing,
once only:

He-e! The Ani-Tsaguhi, the Ani-Tsaguhi,
I want to lay them low on the ground.
The Ani-Tsaguhi, the Ani-Tsaguhi,
I want to lay them low on the ground—*Yu!*

Both the Cherokee and the Creek sing their children lullabies that hunters have heard mother bears singing to their cubs, telling them how to elude the hunters, or remembering the days before they were bears.

The Creek also tell a sad story about a man who turned into a snake.

Two men once went to war, and one of them fell sick. So they returned home. On the way they made camp, and the one who was sick said, "There is something I must eat, or I shall die."

"What?" asked his friend.

"Fish," said the other.

So the friend left him and went looking for a fish.

While he was gone, the sick man found a place where a tree had been uprooted. The hollow had filled with water, and in this water was a fine fish. He cooked this, ate as much as he wanted, and saved the rest for his friend.

When the friend returned, the sick man said, "You know how much I longed for fish. Well, I found one in the water at the root of that fallen tree. I have saved some for you."

But the friend said, "You eat it." So the sick man finished it up.

Soon after this, night came on, and they lay down on opposite sides of the fire. But in the night the sick man called out and woke his friend.

"What's the matter?" the friend asked.

"I feel strange," said the sick man.

By the flickering firelight, the friend looked at the sick man and saw that he had turned into a snake from the waist down.

"Don't be afraid," said the sick man. "But go and ask my family to come for me." Then the sick man stepped into a little stream nearby. At once, the water bubbled up all around him and became a great boiling spring.

When the man who was not sick reached home, the mother and sisters of his friend thought the friend must have been killed in the war. But the man said, "He is not dead. He has turned into a snake. Come with me, and I will show you."

They all went to the spring, and the snake came up from the middle of the pond. He had blue horns. After circling about, he came to the water's edge, crawled out, and laid his head on his mother's lap. He could no longer speak but only shed tears.

His mother hung his belt and ornaments on his horns. Then he circled the pond and, when he came back seized his youngest sister by the waist and carried her down into the water with him.

Ever after, people have avoided that spring. It is a fearful place.

Most versions of this story say that the man became the first tie-snake, but the mention of his blue horns seems to link him with the horned water snake, which in the Northeast and the Southeast is one of the most feared of all the creatures of the underworld. The Cherokee myth of the Daughter of the Sun has already told how this horned snake, Uktena, was created. In the South as in the North, the horned water snake's great enemy is Thunder, and as Creek myths tell of fights between the tie-snake and Thunder, the horned snake and the tie-snake must be the same kind of creature.

The interplay of the forces of above and below on this middle earth is a constant theme, not just in battles between forces such as Thunder and Uktena but in the stories told about human beings. Girls marry stars; men go up to the sky to visit the One Sitting Above; a boy is adopted by the moon. A story told by the Alabama Indians about a canoe that comes down from the sky dramatizes the lure and the perils of contact between the realms.

Some of the sky people came down in a canoe, singing and laughing. When they reached the earth, they got out and played ball on the prairie. When the game was over, they got into the canoe and went back up to the sky. One man saw it all happen, and he wondered who these carefree people were.

They had enjoyed themselves so much that they came back the next day. This time the man was waiting for them, hidden behind a tree. Again they played ball. This time the ball was thrown near where the man was hiding, and one of the sky girls ran to fetch it. As she ran past him, he seized her and carried her off. The other sky people did not know what had happened to her. After a while, they returned to their canoe, and went back to the sky, still singing.

The sky girl married the man, and they had three children. But she never forgot her home in the sky, and behind her husband's back she fashioned herself a dugout canoe. Then she told the children, "Tell your father you are hungry. Ask him to go and hunt deer."

The father started off but did not go far before he returned home. The mother told the children, "Say, 'Father, we need to eat. Go farther off, and kill a deer for us.'"

When he did, the mother and the children got into the canoe and started up into the sky, singing. But the man came running back and pulled the canoe down to the ground, for it was too heavy-laden to rise fast enough.

After that the mother made another, smaller, canoe and put it beside the first. Again she told the children to ask their father to go hunting. When he was gone, she got into the large canoe and the children got into the small one, and they started upward, singing.

The father came running back and managed to catch hold of the children's canoe and pull it back to the ground. But he could only watch as his wife ascended into the sky, singing as she went.

The children pined for their mother, and at last the father agreed to go with them to look for her. They all got into the small canoe and, although it was heavy-laden, it sailed up into the sky.

There they came to the lodge of an old woman. The man told her, "We have come because the children are missing their mother."

She told him, "She is over there, dancing."

Then the old woman cooked some small squashes for them to eat and gave pieces to each of them. They thought, "There isn't enough for all of us." But every time they ate a piece, another appeared in its place. They ate until they were full, but there was still plenty of food left. Then the old woman broke a corncob into pieces, and gave a piece to each of them.

They went on and came to where people were dancing. The children could see their mother, but she could not see them. The first child threw a piece of corncob at her but did not hit her. She passed among them, running. The second child threw a piece of corncob at her but just missed. "What's that smell?" she said as she passed through on the run.

Anonymous
Poling Canoes
Mikasuki Seminole
1920

Flat-bottom dugout canoes could be either punted with a pole or propelled with a paddle. They were commonly used throughout the Southeast, as opposed to the lighter birchbark canoes of the Northeast. The Seminole creator is known as Breath Maker; his son Gives Everything gave the Seminoles the three medicine bundles that are the sacred property of the three divisions of the tribe. The power of the medicine bundles is renewed at the Green Corn Dance, the harvest festival at which a new fire is started for the coming year. The fire is lit by the "breath master," at the center of a square formed by logs pointing north, south, east, and west. The logs are gradually pushed in as they burn.

But when the third child threw, the corn hit her, and she said, "My children!" and came running up to them.

They all got into the canoes and came back to this world.

Sometime later the man went hunting once more, and the wife and children got into the big canoe and went back up to the sky, singing. When the father came home and found them gone, he couldn't bear it. He got into the other canoe and steered it up into the sky. But when he had gone way up high, he turned round to take a last look at the earth and toppled out of the canoe. He fell to the ground and was killed.

But the wife and children, at least, will still be singing and dancing across the arch of the sky when the disk of this earth slips loose from its tethers and capsizes the rest of us into the sea.

4 THE PLAINS

The Ojibwe of the Northeast believe that the sun is the palace of the Great Spirit, who made the world; the nations of the Southeast revere the power of the sun in their annually renewed sacred fires. For the buffalo hunters of the Plains, such as the Sioux, Blackfoot, and Cheyenne, the sun is so important that it became virtually identical to the creative power known to the Sioux as Wakan Tanka, the Great Mystery.

Wakan Tanka is hard to define, partly because the concept itself is fluid and, as the translation suggests, mysterious. Often it is used to mean something like "holy." Good Seat, a Lakota, told James R. Walker, "How the world was made is Wakan Tanka. How men used to talk to animals is Wakan Tanka." The sun is chief of the sixteen benevolent powers—among them Rock, Thunder, and Earth—that control the world, and were known collectively as the Four Times Four. Together they are Wakan Tanka. In addition to the Four Times Four, who are all good, there are many bad gods, of whom the chief is Iya, the Evil Giant, whose brother Iktomi, the Spider Man, originally the god of wisdom, became the Sioux trickster. Both Iya and Iktomi are the children of Inyan, the Rock, who is considered the primal source of all things.

The ancient Romans dedicated altars to "the unknown god," and Wakan Tanka is scarcely more clearly defined. In many instances Wakan Tanka is spoken of as a single being. Wakan Tanka is the maker of all, and a typical Sioux prayer might say simply, "Wakan Tanka, pity me." And so while Wakan Tanka is revered in many ways—for instance, in special rocks charged with sacred power—

Anonymous
Sun Dance
Ponca 1894

The dancers are ranged in a circle around the center pole; a medicine man is seated on the ground within the circle. Many are blowing on bone whistles, and two are holding up hoops twined with greenery. The hoops are a symbol of continuity and wholeness: the Plains Indians envisaged each nation as a hoop. The Lakota medicine man Black Elk said, "Everything an Indian does is in a circle, and that is because the Power of the World always works in circles, and everything tries to be round."

it is not surprising that the Great Mystery should be particularly celebrated in its most visible form, the sun, "the strongest of all mysterious *wakan* powers." In the words of Chased by Bears, who was twice Leader of the Dancers in the Sun Dance, "Greatest of all is the sun, without which we could not live."

The Sun Dance is a four-day ceremony that was held annually, essentially to ensure health, strength, and good fortune for the coming year. It was once banned but is now undergoing a revival. The various Plains nations celebrate it in different ways. A tree is cut to form the Sun Dance pole and erected with offerings of tobacco and a buffalo skull at the center of the Sun Dance lodge. Dancers circle the pole and salute the sun. They may fulfill vows by piercing their skin in self-torture or dance until they fall unconscious, and may, in return, receive a vision. In essence, the Sun Dance is a petition of reverence and submission to the universal power that is greater than man.

The Sun Dance spread among the Plains nations in the early nineteenth century. Many of its features recall the Okeepa, or Buffalo Dance, of the Mandan, a highly complex ritual that was observed and recorded by George Catlin shortly before the Mandan nation was all but wiped out by a smallpox epidemic. It dramatized the victory of good over evil and ensured a plentiful supply of buffalo for the coming year. The connection between buffalo and the sun is strong; the Sioux say that Buffalo and Sun sit together in council every night.

The Mandan believed that they were the first people created and that originally they lived inside the earth, where they grew vines.

> One day an adventurous Mandan youth named Na-ci-i climbed up a vine and through a hole in the earth to the place where the Mandan village of large earth

lodges stood, in the upper Missouri. There he killed a buffalo and found it good to eat. He went back and told the others what he had seen, and many of them followed him back up the vine, including his brother, the chief, and his sister. One heavily pregnant woman was told by the chief not to go up. But she was so curious that she could not resist, and when no one was looking, she climbed up the vine. She was nearly at the top when the vine broke under her weight, and sent her tumbling to the ground. And after that, no more people could ascend to the earth, nor could those who had climbed up ever go back down.

The Mandan believed that some people still lived beneath the earth, which was supported either by the Great Turtle or by four turtles, one at each of the cardinal points. The place where the people first emerged onto the earth, at the mouth of Heart River, was the very center of the world, which was created from the primeval

ocean by First Creator and Lone Man with the help of a mudhen earth diver. First Creator then became Coyote. Lone Man was reborn as a Mandan, and traveled in his magic canoe performing miracles. He left a sacred cedar post, representing his body, to protect the Mandan from all harm.

The Mandan thought that if they did not dance the Okeepa, a flood would come and destroy humanity, as it had once before, when only Lone Man survived.

At the start of the Okeepa, a figure covered in white clay representing Lone Man entered the village carrying a sacred pipe and calling to the Great Spirit. After consecrating the medicine lodge, he called at each lodge in turn, telling the story of the flood and receiving gifts of edged tools, like those he had used to make his canoe; these were later thrown into the river as offerings.

At the climax of the dance, a figure covered in black

grease, representing O-ke-hée-de, the Foolish One, entered the village, to be pacified by the medicine man with the sacred pipe and finally vanquished by one of the women. This woman was said to hold the power of creation and of life and death, and to be the mother of the buffalo.

The buffalo was at the heart of Plains mythology. At the beginning of the last century, Roaming Chief, hereditary chief of the Chaui Pawnee, gave an account of creation that demonstrates this. Roaming Chief told the ethnologists George A. Dorsey and James R. Murie (himself a Pawnee) how Tirawa the creator made the heavens and earth and brought the first woman and the first man into being with "the sound of his voice."

"The earth I give you," Tirawa told them, "and you are to call her 'mother,' for she gives birth to all things."

Tirawa told the first couple how to build a timber lodge, with four posts, in the northeast, northwest, southwest, and southeast, to represent the four gods who hold up the heavens. The entrance of the lodge must face the east, to allow the building to "breathe as if human." In the west they should make a small mound for an altar, and place upon it a buffalo skull, through which Tirawa could "live with you and communicate with you." Above the altar, they were to hang the medicine bundle he gave them.

Tirawa then taught them the Starisu, the Woman's Dance. If it was performed every spring, Tirawa would always send buffalo to feed the people. The story of the dance is itself part of the ritual, told to the dancers by the chief before the ceremony.

The people were starving. The young man who was responsible for the dance had given it, but still no buffalo had come. So he went away to seek an answer. He

Edward S. Curtis
Sacred Turtle Drums
Mandan 1908

The creator Lone Man made four sacred turtle drums for the Mandan, which were beaten by four elders during the Okeepa, or Buffalo Dance. The people adorned three drums with black eagle feathers and the fourth with spotted feathers. The fourth drum was so angry at being treated differently that it rushed off and dived into the river, so now there are only three. When Edward Curtis photographed these two drums, their keeper, Packs Wolf, said anxiously, "Do not turn them over; if you do, all the people will die." The drums are made of buffalo skin. According to Curtis, each one houses a spirit buffalo; according to George Catlin, the drums contain water gathered from the four corners of the world as the great flood subsided.

was guided by the Moon to a hilly country, and there on a hillside he came to a cave.

In the cave sat an old woman, who said, "I am the Moon. I brought you here. The people are starving. Tirawa promised he would send you buffalo, but there are not enough buffalo on earth. We will have to call up some of the buffalo that live under the ground. For now, take these pieces of fat back to the people. Let them chew on the fat, and that will give them the strength to endure. For the buffalo are far away, and it will be some time before they can answer my call."

The young man took the fat to the people, and everybody chewed a little of it. Then he went back to the cave and this time found a young woman there. She gave him gambling sticks and said, "Let the men of your people play with these sticks, so that they will not think about eating." Then she gave him a basket full of plum seeds, and said, "Give these to the women. Let them play with this basket and these seeds, so that they will not think about eating." And then she gave him two pieces of dried meat, and said, "Give these to the children, so that they may eat."

The young man took these gifts back to the people and then returned to the cave. There he found the same young woman, and she told him to stand by the entrance of the cave while she called the buffalo. She called:

> Lihoo-oo-oo-oo!
> Lihoo-oo-oo-oo!
> Lihoo-oo-oo-oo!
> Lihoo-oo-oo-oo!

At the last call, the buffalo rushed out from the cave. The young man returned to the people and told them there were now buffalo on the prairie, and the people went and killed many buffalo.

So long as the Woman's Dance is performed correctly, it will call more buffalo from beneath the earth and keep the people from starvation. Such rituals (many of which are beautifully recorded in James R. Murie's *Ceremonies of the Pawnee*) are necessary in order to maintain the

world, by celebrating and reenacting the time of creation.

The gifts of the Moon—who is seen as both an old woman and a young one, in recognition of the moon's ability to wax and wane—are particularly interesting. The sticks enabled the men to keep score in the hoop-and-pole game, which was given to the people by Tirawa and which is intimately concerned with the buffalo hunt. The myth of the game's origin was told only in a lodge where medicine bundles were kept or during a buffalo hunt to honor the spirits of the buffalo that were killed. The story tells how, after the game was played for the very first time, one of the players made love to a young woman who was really Buffalo Woman.

Some time later she gave birth to a calf, who was always crying for his father. When the young man answered the calf's call, the bulls challenged him to identify the calf. If he could not, they would kill him. All the calves were arranged in a row, and the young man walked up and down past them three times but was unable to tell which was his. Then he saw one of the calves wink. He pointed to it, saying, "This is my son." So the buffalo bulls let him go. He went back to the village and told his people, "In four days the buffalo will come in great numbers; we will kill them and have plenty of meat, and fat with which to grease the poles for our game."

The gifts for the women relate to the basket dice game, a game of chance played with a basket containing seven plum seeds. A myth told by Woman Cleanse the People, keeper of the skull medicine bundle, gives an account of the game's origin and explains its symbolism.

When the creation was going on, the gods made two images of humans out of mud, one a girl and the other a boy. In time, the images seemed to wake up.

A bow and some arrows were given to the boy, so that they could live by killing animals for food.

The gods couldn't decide whether they should have darkness or light to live in. "Let's see which animal he kills first," the gods said.

The animals went past the young man in the dark. Some were black, some were white. He couldn't tell. But he held his fire until the last one and shot it through the heart. It was spotted white and black, so the gods created both day and night. As the animal died, the first day dawned.

One night the man and the woman were sitting in their grass lodge when they heard the sound of singing and dancing. The next day the young man went hunting in the forest, and there he found a lodge and a small field of corn. He went home and fetched the young woman, and together they approached the lodge.

A woman came out and asked them to come in. She

Edward S. Curtis
Buffalo Dancers
Cheyenne 1927

These female dancers are wearing horned buffalo-pelt headdresses and have ritual whistles hanging from their necks. The Buffalo Dance was part of the preparation for a buffalo hunt; dancers imitated buffalo to bring success to the hunt. The Cheyenne were enabled to kill buffalo by Falling Star, the son of a Cheyenne girl who married a star. He disguised himself as a buffalo and killed a white crow that had been warning the buffalo of the hunters' approach.

51

was the Moon. Inside was an altar, and seated at the altar were four old men who were painted with red clay. There were also many girl children in the lodge, singing and dancing. They were the Moon's daughters, the stars. The woman told the young man and woman to learn the dances and the songs. Then she brought in corn and they all ate, and the young man and woman were given seeds to take home with them.

After the dancing, the young man and woman were taught the basket game. The four old men were singing. They were Wind, Clouds, Lightning, and Thunder. In front of them, in the west, a woman was dancing, holding a basket. She was Evening Star, the goddess of storms.

To the east of Evening Star were four dancing girls, the daughters of the Big Black Meteoric Star. who stands northeast in the heavens and who gave the medicine men all their bundles and mysteries. As they danced, they moved to the west and threw into the basket carried by Evening Star the things that they were holding. These were two swan necks and two fawn skins, representing the four gods in the west. This ended the dance.

Then the young man and woman were given the basket and seven plum seeds, and were told to make marks on the plum seeds representing the stars. "This basket represents the Moon," said Evening Star. "She is the mother of the stars, and Tirawa sent us down to earth in the basket of the Moon to teach you how to live."

Evening Star told them that the basket itself must be made of willow, for the earth is filled with timber. They must not use a knife to make it, just water and mud. "Everything you need has been put in the earth, and what is beyond your power you may obtain from the Big Black Meteoric Star." She taught them how to play the basket dice game, and how to keep count with the twelve sticks that represent the twelve stars in a circle above the heavens, who sit as chiefs in council.

When the stars saw that the people understood what they must do in this life, they jumped into their basket and went back up into the heavens.

The Blackfoot tell how the laws of the world were established in this creation time. The land and animals were created by Na'pi, Old Man, who then made the first people out of clay. It was the first woman who, seeing life stretching on before her, brought death into the world.

The first woman walked down to the river with Old Man. She asked him, "Will we always live? Will there be no end to it?"

"I never thought of that," he answered. "We will have to decide. I will take this buffalo chip and throw it in the river. If it floats, then when people die, they will come back to life; but if it sinks, then there will be an end to them." He threw the chip into the river, and it floated.

But the woman turned and picked up a stone, saying, "I will throw this into the river. If it floats, we will

Fred E. Miller
Women Playing a Game of Chance
Crow c. 1900

Variants of the Basket Dice Game were played by the women of many Plains tribes. Plum stones variously marked with moons and stars were tossed like dice from a basket or bowl, and the scores added up according to how the stones fell; the woman shown here appears to be simply shaking dice in her cupped hands. Sticks were used to keep score. The game was not played for money but for valuables such as necklaces, moccasins, earrings, and paint. Plains men played a gambling game known as Hiding the Stone, in which players had to guess under which moccasin a stone had been hidden. The men played for higher stakes, often horses or weapons.

53

always live; but if it sinks, people must die, and live only in the memory of their friends."

The woman threw the stone into the water, and it sank.

"There," said Old Man. "You have chosen. There will be an end to them."

It was not many nights after this that the woman's child died, and she cried bitterly for it. She went to Old Man and said, "I've changed my mind. Let the first law you suggested be the law."

But he said, "No. What is made law must be law. We will undo nothing that we have done. The child is dead. It cannot be changed. People will have to die."

In the beginning, say the Blackfoot, people were poor and naked. Old Man had to show them how to gather roots and berries and catch small animals and birds, and he also taught them the healing properties of the herbs. The people had no weapons, and the buffalo hunted them.

One day as Old Man was traveling over the country he had made, he saw some of his children lying dead, torn to pieces and partly eaten by the buffalo. "This will not do," he said. "I will change this. The people shall eat the buffalo." And so he gave the people bows and arrows and taught them how to hunt the buffalo.

The Arikara tell how Buffalo Woman travels all over this world, searching for buffalo and summoning them. She walks around the symbolic world of the medicine lodge, from post to post, each time changing her moccasins; and by the time she arrives at each of the four posts, her moccasins are worn out with traveling. Buffalo Woman never eats meat—she likes only corn; conversely, Corn Woman never eats corn but loves meat.

Whether the first humans on this earth were brought into being by the sound of their creator's voice, were shaped from clay, or emerged from the world under the ground, the care of the creator—Man Never Known on

Earth, as the Wichita term him—remains the same. It is he who provides both corn and buffalo, and establishes natural law.

The Arapaho origin myth tells how at first there was nothing but water and waterfowl, and then the Grandfather became aware of a pipe floating on the water, and on the pipe were the first Arapaho. With the help of the duck and turtle, who brought up mud from the bottom, the Grandfather created a world in the shape of a turtle for these people to live in. The Arapaho call the pipe Father.

Archaeological evidence shows that pipes have been used by Native Americans for four thousand years. The gift of the sacred pipe (sometimes called by the French name, calumet) and the rituals surrounding its care and use feature in the mythologies of many nations, and none more so than the Sioux.

The sacred pipe was the gift to the Sioux of White Buffalo Maiden, who is identified with Wohpe, the goddess of beauty and pleasure, the daughter of Skan, the sky. White Buffalo Maiden told the Sioux that when they smoked, she would be present and hear their prayers and would take them to Wakan Tanka. Thomas Tyon, an Oglala Lakota who recorded traditions and beliefs for James R. Walker, the white physician at the Pine Ridge reservation, wrote that, "the pipe is very *wakan*. If a people quarrel, then they make peace using the pipe." For the Lakota, Tyon said, "the pipe is their heart."

This remains true today. The sacred pipe bundle containing the Buffalo Calf Pipe brought by White Buffalo Maiden is, in the words of Raymond J. DeMallie and Douglas R. Parks, "the most sacred possession of the Lakota people and the very soul of their religious life." Crow Dog, a Sicanga (Brulé) Lakota medicine man, says, "As the pipe goes around, every puff is a prayer."

The famous Oglala holy man Black Elk devoted the last years of his life to the recording of seven rites of the sacred pipe. They are: the Keeping of the Soul, which purifies the souls of the dead; the Sweat Lodge, which purifies the souls of the living; Crying for a Vision; the Sun Dance; the Making of Relatives; Preparing for Womanhood; and Throwing the Ball, the Sioux sacred ball game.

Alexander Gardner
Fort Laramie Peace Talks
Lakota **1868**

This is the only known photograph of an Indian smoking a council pipe. The smoker is Man Careful of His Horses, a chief of the Oglala Sioux and a celebrated warrior, who was the representative of the war chief Red Cloud at the Fort Laramie talks. Red Cloud himself refused to attend the peace talks until the U.S. Army abandoned the forts they had built along the Powder River. A copy of the treaty had to be left at the fort for him to sign. As soon as the troops marched out, Red Cloud and his men burned the forts to the ground. But the victory was not without cost; though the military did withdraw from tribal lands, the conditions of the treaty were not properly understood by the Indians who signed it. They did, however, understand that all might not be as it seemed. The Oglala chief Four Bears told the Peace Commissioners, "You say that you will protect us for thirty years, but I do not believe it."

White Buffalo Maiden not only gave the Sioux the pipe and taught them the seven rites, but she also periodically returns to the Sioux to renew the sacred contract between her and the people. For instance, in June 1974, another Oglala holy man, Frank Fools Crow, told Thomas E. Mails, "At this very moment, she is walking about the United States in the company of another young woman. This is a bad omen, which tells us that the end times are upon us."

One Sioux myth says that in a cave in the Badlands there is a wrinkled old woman who has been working on a blanket strip of porcupine quills for her buffalo robe for a thousand years or more. Every now and then she must lay down her work in order to stir the soup that has been bubbling on her fire since time began. When she does, the huge black dog that lies at her feet tears the porcupine quills from the blanket strip with his teeth. So her quillwork is never finished. But if she ever manages to complete her blanket strip, the world will come to an end.

For the Cheyenne, the end will come with a terrible crash, as Mrs. Medicine Bull told Richard Erdoes. In the north, she explained, there is a great pole, like an enormous sacred Sun Dance pole, and this pole is what holds up the earth. Through all time, the Great White Grandfather Beaver of the north has been gnawing at the pole, and more than half of it is already gnawed through. Once he has gnawed all the way through, the pole will topple, and the world will crash into the great nothingness. When the Beaver gets angry, he gnaws even more furiously and the pole is whittled away even faster. That is why the Cheyenne never eat beaver, or even touch a beaver pelt. They don't want to upset the Great White Grandfather Beaver. They want the world to last a little while longer.

The Pawnee say that when the first race of humans was destroyed by the great flood, Tirawa the creator placed a great buffalo bull in the northwest to hold back the floodwaters. Every year this buffalo drops one hair. When all the hairs have fallen off, the end will come for the present race. But Tirawa will not send another flood.

Young Bull, a Pitahauirat Pawnee medicine man, remembered his grandmother's words. She told him that the stars will sit in council and select a day when all things shall cease to be. Various signs will foretell the end.

> My grandchild, some of the signs have come to pass. The stars have fallen among the people, but the Morning Star is still good to us, for we continue to live. The Moon has turned black several times, but we know that the Morning Star said that whenever the Moon turned black, it would be a sign that some great chief or warrior was to die.
>
> My grandchild, we are told by the old people that the Morning Star and the Evening Star placed people upon this earth. The North Star and the South Star will end all things. All commands were given in the west and these commands were carried out in the east. The command for the ending of all things will be given by the North Star, and the South Star will carry out the commands.
>
> Our people were made by the stars. When the time comes for all things to end, our people will turn into small stars and will fly to the South Star, where they belong. When the time comes for the ending of the world, the stars will again fall to earth. They will mix among the people, for it will be a message to the people to get ready to be turned into stars.

5 THE SOUTHWEST

The Southwest contains both desert nations (such as the Pima, Papago, and Navajo), and the pueblo peoples (such as the Hopi and Zuñi). Each individual nation has woven a complex web of myth and ritual, often sharing some aspects with its neighbors but always taking an intensely individual form, uniquely tailored by the forces of culture, history, and geography.

The story of the emergence of mankind from below the earth is one common denominator of Southwest myth. The most complicated of the emergence myths, that of the Hopi, tells of four worlds to date and prophesies a fifth world in the near future, when only the Hopi and their homeland will survive the "Purification Day."

The Keresan pueblo tribes tell emergence stories that are fairly typical, except that the creation and shaping of the world is very much a female affair. It was Thinking Woman, they say, who thought the world into being. Beneath the earth, and identified with it, is Iatiku, the breath of life, who is the Corn Mother. Iatiku has two daughters, to whom she gives baskets filled with seeds and images with which to bring life to the world: as they emerge from below, singing their creation song, the things they sprinkle from their baskets come to life.

The first daughter is usually also called Iatiku, and mother and daughter are essentially two aspects of the same goddess—one who comes up to this world with her gift of life, and one who remains below and to whom the dead return. Iatiku is the mother of the Indians. She was responsible for the creation of the world as it is—even of such elements as fun and laughter.

She is regarded as the breath of life. The second daughter is the mother of the whites. At first she did not have a name, but then Iatiku saw that her basket was more richly filled than her sister's, so she was named Nautsiti, meaning "more of everything in her basket."

Thinking Woman, who created the world from the web of her thoughts, can be identified with Spider Woman, an important figure in all Southwest mythology; when Thinking Woman took bodily form, it was as a spider. During Iatiku's contests with her sister, Nautsiti, Thinking Woman sat on her shoulder and whispered advice into her ear.

According to the Hopi, it was Spider Woman who made the first people out of clay. She made them in pairs, male and female, but one time she forgot and made only a man. Later she made a single woman and sent her out to look for the single man. But when they finally found each other, they argued all the time and eventually separated. That was the beginning of all quarrels between husbands and wives.

Spider Woman taught the peoples how to weave and, say the Hopi, wove the moon from white cotton. She has the power to give and take life. Navajos never kill spiders, and any child who does so is expected to have crooked teeth in adulthood, because Spider Woman's needle-sharp teeth are said to slant backward, to stop her prey from escaping. To encourage Navajo girls to become tireless weavers, spiderwebs are rubbed on their arms. And when a Navajo woman uses Spider Woman's knowledge to weave a rug, she must weave a break into the pattern at the end, so that her soul may come back out to her and not be trapped in the web.

The myths of the Navajo also tell how Spider Woman helped the hero twins Monster Slayer and Born for Water find their father, the Sun. They entered his lodge

James Mooney
Kachinas
Hopi 1893

Kachinas are spirits who mediate between the human world and the spirit world. They are represented in Hopi rituals by masked dancers, and Hopi children are introduced to them by the gift of beautifully carved kachina dolls. Hopis believe that those who have lived a good life will become kachinas and will return to their home villages as clouds. These kachinas are overseeing the initiation of Hopi children into adult life in the Powamu ceremony. The two standing at the front are Hehea, or Crooked Mouth, kachinas, ancient forms of the kachina who play a role in many ceremonies, both public and secret. At the back are two Natashku—scary kachinas who go from house to house demanding food. They are Habai wuhti and her husband, Natashku naamu, wearing an animal mask with a crest of turkey feathers.

63

and hid among some rugs. When the Sun came home and hung the sun up on the west wall of his house, he sensed their presence. He unfurled first the rug of dawn, then the rug of the daytime sky, then the rug of twilight, and finally the blue-black rug of the night sky, before spilling the twins out onto the floor. When Monster Slayer and Born for Water convinced him that they were his sons, he armed them with magic arrows so that they could make the earth safe for humanity by destroying the monsters that previously ruled it. Though these heroes killed many evil creatures, they could never slay Old Age, Cold, and Hunger.

The hero twins, whose exploits are told throughout the Southwest, are the children of the most important Navajo goddess, Changing Woman. Like Iatiku, she represents the life force, and she created the Navajo people from the mountain soil bundle brought by First Man from the world below. It was from this medicine bundle that the current world was created.

Changing Woman is the daughter of Long Life Boy and Happiness Girl. She was brought to life by Talking God from a turquoise image and raised by First Man and First Woman. She is the essence of life, and her existence is an endless cycle of change, in which she grows old and then young again with the seasons.

Navajo myths are vibrantly expressed in the ceremonies of song, prayer, dance, and ritual known as chantways. The most famous of these is the healing ritual known as the Yeibichai, or the Nightway. The rituals involve beautiful sand paintings, which are both created and destroyed as part of the ritual. The Navajo name of such paintings means "place where the gods come and go."

Each chantway expresses the myth of how the healing knowledge of the specific ritual was acquired. The myth

of the Mountainway, for instance, tells in part of a young Navajo man named Reared Within the Mountain.

One day, Reared Within the Mountain went out hunting and was captured by a band of Ute warriors. They wanted him to teach them the secret of stalking deer, which he had learned from his father. If he shared his knowledge with them, they would spare his life.

Reared Within the Mountain initiated two of the Utes into the secret, teaching them how to make a sweat lodge to purify themselves, and how to make a mask from the head of a slain deer and imitate the movements of the animal.

So his life was spared for now, but Reared Within the Mountain remained a captive of the Utes, tied up in a great lodge. While the Utes held council on what to do with him, various beings came to him—a strange old woman, and a spirit in an owl mask—warning him to do something to save himself. Three times he heard "Hu'hu'hu'hu'," the distinctive call of Talking God, grandfather of the gods and god of the dawn and the eastern sky. At dawn Talking God entered the lodge on a bolt of white lightning through the smokehole, and told Reared Within the Mountain that the Utes had decided to put him to death. He had to leave, taking with him the bags filled with embroideries and tobacco from the pouches that were lying near the fire.

With Talking God's help, Reared Within the Mountain freed himself, took the embroideries and tobacco, and fled, following the call of an owl. The Utes pursued him, but when he reached an impassable canyon, Talking God blew out a rainbow with his breath to make a bridge for Reared Within the Mountain to cross.

On his way home, Reared Within the Mountain had a series of encounters with Holy People, who made him as beautiful as they are, and taught him the secrets of the Mountainway. When he finally reached his home, he taught these secrets to the people. But Reared Within the Mountain himself could not stay. He found that after his experiences the smell of human beings was disgusting to him, so he returned to live with the Holy People. He told his brother, "You will never see me again. But when the showers pass and the thunder peals, you will say, 'There is the voice of my elder brother.'"

The Mountainway songs call on Holy People such as Daylight Boy and Daylight Girl, and trace their beautiful journey from the house of dawn to the house of evening light. The sick person for whom the ceremony is held appeals for help from Reared Within the Mountain, in terms that make clear how the whole nine-day ritual is designed not simply to heal an individual but to restore and renew the world. The patient chants:

Reared Within the Mountain!
Lord of the Mountain!
Young Man!
Chieftain!
I have made your sacrifice.

Simeon Schwernberger
The Patient on the Sand Painting
Navajo 1906

The healing ceremony known as the Yeibichai, or the Nightway Chant, lasts nine days. The first eight are conducted in private inside a traditional Navajo log hogan (which represents the world), while the ninth is a public spectacle held outside under the winter moon. The masked man sitting on the rug represents Talking God, the most important character in the Nightway. He is the yeibichai, *the grandfather of the gods. The yei are the Navajo equivalent of the Hopi kachinas or the Apache hactcin; the word "yei" is often translated as spirits or as Holy People.*

I have prepared a smoke for you.
My feet restore for me.
My legs restore for me.
My body restore for me.
My mind restore for me.
My voice restore for me.
Restore all for me in beauty.
Make beautiful all that is before me.
Make beautiful all that is behind me.
Make beautiful my words.
It is done in beauty.
It is done in beauty.
It is done in beauty.
It is done in beauty.

The Pima-Papago creator is called Earth Doctor, or Earth Medicine Man. He is envisaged not as a spider, like the Keresan creator, Thinking Woman, but as a great butterfly. At first there was no earth, and no water—just Earth Doctor, floating serene and alone in the great darkness. Frank Russell recorded a Pima creation song from Thin Leather that tells how the universe was brought into being. Earth Doctor first shaped the round world and then made the mountains and the mesas. He threw blocks of ice into the sky to make the sun and moon, and a spray of water to make the stars.

After this, Earth Doctor fluttered down to earth and there made the first men from the dust on his breast. But the people he made were too quarrelsome, and they annoyed him so much that he decided to destroy them all. He let the sky fall on them. Only Earth Doctor himself and his helper, Buzzard, survived, fleeing through a hole in the sky.

The same thing happened two more times, and it was only on the fourth attempt that Earth Doctor made the earth as it is today. At first the earth was all mountains, and there was no water for people to drink, but Earth Doctor sent Buzzard to fly through the mountains and

Edward S. Curtis
House God
Navajo **1904**

House God lives in caves and other sacred places on Navajo land, such as Broad Rock in the Canyon de Chelly. He is the god of home and farm. He often accompanies Talking God in Navajo myths and is regarded as the god of the west and the sunset, while Talking God is the god of the east and the dawn. The face of his mask is blue, representing the sky; it is trimmed with a fan of eagle feathers, a bunch of owl feathers, and a collar of spruce. According to the Navajo origin legend, the children of First Man and First Woman were taken away to the eastern mountain by the gods and kept there for four days. When they returned, they had masks, like the ones Talking God and House God now wear, and wore them when they prayed for all good things, such as rain or crops.

carve valleys with his wings, so that the rivers could flow over the earth.

The Moon and the Sun had a child and, after it was born, left it on the earth to look after itself. That child was Coyote. He made his way to the house of Earth Doctor and Buzzard, and they took him in. And the Sky and the Earth had a child, and that was Elder Brother.

Edward S. Curtis
Starting a Fire
Apache 1906

The White Mountain Apache tell how long ago only the privileged few, of which the chief was Squirrel, had fire. Coyote used witch power on Squirrel and made him sick, and then suggested to the other fire people (the hawk family) that they have a dance to cure him. They danced around a fire, carefully catching each stray spark and returning it to the fire. Because Coyote had suggested the dance, they allowed him to join in. He had tied a bunch of dry bark under his tail, and when this caught fire, he ran away. He spread fire across the dry grass and brush by shaking his tail from side to side.

He came from the north, and the others welcomed him, calling him Younger Brother. But he insisted that he was the oldest, so in order to please him they called him Elder Brother.

Elder Brother took over from Earth Doctor at this point as the ruler of creation. Assisted by Earth Doctor and Coyote, he made animals, birds, and plants, and shaped new people from clay.

The time came, however, when the people decided to do away with Elder Brother. They resented the way he kept tempting their girls to be his wives, and then tiring of them and sending them back. They tried all kinds of ways to kill him. They beat him with clubs. They set fire to him. They cut him up into pieces and boiled him in a pot. They tied him up and threw him over a cliff. They drowned him in a whirlpool. But every time he just got up and walked away. Then Buzzard, jealous of Elder Brother, offered the people his aid.

"You won't be able to kill him," Buzzard said. "He may be too powerful even for me to kill. He has power over the winds and the animals, and he knows everything that is happening on the earth and in the sky. But I have power something like his. Come to my house, and I will show you."

The people went to Buzzard's house and found he had created a whole miniature world. It had a sun, moon, and stars. It was just like our world. He made it with the power Earth Doctor gave him, when Earth Doctor made Buzzard out of the shadow of his eye to be his helper. And then the people believed that if anyone could kill Elder Brother, Buzzard could.

Buzzard climbed the zigzag ladders of his house and flew up through the smoke hole to watch the sunrise. As soon as the sun was up, Buzzard flew toward it, higher and higher, until he could see Elder Brother's heart. He flew right to the Sun himself and asked for the Sun's help. "There is a very bad person on the earth," he said, "and I want to kill him. Please

lend me your bow." And the Sun lent Buzzard his bow.

Buzzard shot at Elder Brother with a sun-ray arrow, and Elder Brother felt his heart get warm. He shot again, and Elder Brother felt his heart become hot. He tried to cool himself in a pool of water, but the water was boiling hot. Elder Brother went to a rock that was always cold, but just before he reached it the rock burst with the heat. Then he ran to a shady tree, but just before he reached it the tree burst into flame.

Now it was noon, and Elder Brother felt as if the whole world was burning up. He ran to a post, which he had made with his power, that was hollow and cool inside. But just before he reached it, Buzzard fired again, and Elder Brother fell down dead.

Elder Brother lay dead for four years. The first thing that he saw when he recovered consciousness was the wonderful miniature world that Buzzard made, and so he understood that it was Buzzard who almost killed him. Earth Doctor sent the four winds to gather him up, and bring him home. When the winds dropped him, Earth Doctor gathered Elder Brother tenderly in his arms, like a sick child.

When he was fully recovered, Elder Brother went down to the world below, and led the people there up onto the earth, where they fell upon the ungrateful humans and destroyed them. These new people were the Pima-Papago, and this tale of vengeance is their myth of emergence. One of the first things they did on earth was to catch Buzzard and bring him, with his hands and feet bound together, for judgment. They wanted to kill him, but he talked them out of it. "You never know, I might be useful to you," he said. And by singing and dancing, Buzzard held the people so spellbound that they forgot he was their enemy.

Elder Brother went to Earth Doctor and got him to take away Buzzard's power, so although he survived, he could no longer make a miniature world to play with or be a threat to this world. He must live on carrion, and anyone can kill him.

One version of the Pima creation myth tells how when Elder Brother made human beings, the first ones he made were the warlike Apache. Displeased, Elder Brother threw them over the mountain—but that just made them even fiercer. The last people were, of course, the Pima, who were given special powers—in particular, the power to make rain.

The word "Apache" is the Zuñi word for "enemy." Their own name for themselves is Inde, which, like most of the true names of the Indian nations, simply means "people." One White Mountain Apache creation myth tells how in the beginning all was dark, until a disk

appeared in the void. In it was the creator, the One Who Lives Above, envisaged as a small bearded man.

As if emerging from a long sleep, the One Who Lives Above rubbed his eyes and face. Then light streamed from his eyes and created the dawn and the sunset. He wiped the sweat from his face and rubbed it from his hands, and it became a shining cloud on which sat Girl Without Parents. Then he wiped his brow again and made Sun God, and again and made Small Boy. These four gods sat together on the cloud, deep in thought.

The cloud was too small for them to live on, so they decided to make the earth. They shook hands and mixed their sweat together, forming it into a ball about the size of a bean. They kicked this ball about, and every time they kicked it, it expanded. Then the One Who

Lives Above told Wind to go inside the ball and blow it up.

When the earth and the sky were made, the One Who Lives Above sent Lightning Maker to circle the world and see what he could find. He returned with three half-made creatures he found in a turquoise shell—two girls and a boy.

The One Who Lives Above built the first sweat lodge, and Girl Without Parents covered it with four clouds. They placed the three creatures in the sweat lodge and sang songs of healing, giving them fingers and toes and faces and bringing them to life. These three creatures were Sky Boy, Earth Daughter, and Pollen Girl.

Soon the world was engulfed by a great flood, but Girl Without Parents led them to safety, in an ark made from a piñon tree, sealed with piñon gum. When they stepped from the ark, the One Who Lives Above told them that his work of creation was complete and that he was leaving them in charge. Lightning Maker was to be responsible for the clouds and water, Sky Boy, for the sky people, Earth Daughter, for the earth people, Pollen Girl, for the health of the earth people, and Girl Without Parents was to be in charge over all.

The Apache culture heroes are Child of the Water and Killer of Enemies, whose adventures ridding the world of monsters are essentially the same as those of the Navajo twins Monster Slayer and Born for Water, or the Little War Gods of the pueblos. Child of the Water is often credited with the creation of human beings. He is the son of the Rain and White Shell Woman, while Killer of Enemies is the child of the Sun and White Painted Woman.

Besides creating the Indians, Child of the Water also made the whites. He created them from two blue-eyed fish, a male and a female, that he found in the ocean. First he lay on the ground and made a tracing of his

body. Then he placed the fish within the outline and transformed them in stages from fish into human beings.

The adventures of all these beings of the early world are the foundation of Apache culture. Apache women still model themselves after White Shell Woman and White Painted Woman, and men after Child of the Water and Killer of Enemies. But the stories about them (which differ from tribe to tribe) do not make up the bulk of Apache myths. Instead, the myths are concerned with the often comic exploits of the trickster Coyote, who is said to have been the last animal to come from beneath the earth at the time of the emergence from the world below.

Holy beings such as Child of the Water laid down the rules of proper living; Coyote defines those rules by breaking them. He is always getting into terrible trouble, but he always escapes—to transgress another day.

Often Coyote gets what he wants by playing on the

greed or gullibility of others, as in the story of how he sold the money tree.

Coyote had a few dollars, but he wanted more. So he stuck the dollars up in a tree, sat down beneath it, and waited for someone to come along. It was a group of white people, prospectors or something.

They saw Coyote sitting under the tree and asked him what he was doing.

"I'm guarding my tree," he said.

"Why?"

"Because this tree is very valuable. It's the only one of its kind."

"The only one of what kind?" they asked.

"Why, the only money tree! Every year, it bears a crop of money. All I have to do is shake the tree and the money drops down. I'm just waiting for it to ripen now."

The prospectors were very excited. "Will you sell us the tree?" they asked. "We'll give you everything we have—horses, packs, blankets, everything."

Coyote sat and thought about it. He acted as if he really didn't want to sell.

At last he agreed to sell them the tree, but on one condition. "Wait till I've gone over that blue mountain before you shake the tree. I just couldn't bear to watch you harvesting all that money."

One of the men said, "Let's see you shake the tree a little before you go, just to prove that money really is going to fall from it."

Coyote gave the tree a little shake, and his few dollars floated down to the ground.

The men agreed, "Sure enough, it does bear money!" So they gave Coyote everything they had and watched him go off with their horses and all their possessions. They waited till he was over the mountain, and then they began to shake that tree as hard as they could. But however hard they shook, no more money fell.

They went looking for Coyote. They ran into him at a camp, but the camp was overrun with coyotes and they couldn't tell which was which. They asked one of them if he had seen anyone come in with a lot of horses. It was Coyote himself. "Sure," he said. "He went that way." And he sent them off in one direction, while he went in the other.

Some people say that one of those foolish prospectors still goes every year to give the money tree a shake, just in case.

6 CALIFORNIA

California is particularly rich in creation myths that tell both of the way the earth was made, and the time before humans, which the Karok call Pikavahairak. The doings of the First People who lived in this creation time are still celebrated today in ceremonies and myths, and the First People themselves are thought to have been transformed into present-day animals, plants, trees, and rocks.

The mythology of the Yurok centers around the adventures of two heroes—Wohpekumeu, a trickster figure who steals salmon and acorns for mankind and lays down the laws of nature, and Pulekukwerek, who established the night sky and slays monsters, making the world safe for humankind—the Real People. Wohpekumeu is so potent with creation that he need only look at a woman to make her pregnant; his ever-renewing lust is his downfall. When he embraces Skate, she refuses to let go, and carries him away across the ocean—hence the meaning of his name, "widower from across the ocean." Pulekukwerek also leaves this world; he goes to a land far away where there is constant dancing.

The adventures of these two culture heroes do not take place in the world of modern man, but in the world of the *woge*, the First People, who, when humanity was created, shyly and sadly retreated into the mountains or over the sea, or turned themselves into animals, birds, rocks, landmarks, or disembodied spirits.

The *woge* took part in the process of creation, forming the geography of the earth and establishing laws of

C. Hart Merriam
Dancers
Pomo 1907

These men are dressed for the Big Head Dance, a ritual of the Kuksu cult, which enables dancers to acquire power by impersonation of and contact with the spirits. The dancers dressed outdoors and were summoned from the roof of the dance house. They entered the dance house separately, in the character of the spirit they represented. The main dance step was an alternate raising of the knees, with the feet violently stamped to the ground; the spirit impersonators also leaped over the ritual drum. The man in the center here is dressed as the Tuya, or Big Head, a male spirit.

marriage and justice, before being supplanted by the new race of humans. "When these human beings came," said Johnny Shortman, a Yurok, "all the *woge* went off to the hills."

The Yurok talk with a sense of yearning and sadness about the *woge*, the people who "instituted everything." They still call on the *woge* in rituals, for even though they retreated from humanity, they are still present in the world and well disposed toward us.

The first human beings, according to the Yurok, were the children of a dog woman, the wife of one of the spirits who originated the ritual Jumping Dance and Deerskin Dance; these spirits are known as "those through whom we live." After she began to have human children, her dog offspring were put out of the house; dogs now follow after men, but men first came from them.

Other Californian mythologies also preserve memories of a world before this one. The Wiyot tell how when Above Old Man first tried to make people, he did not get it right. They could not talk properly, and they were all furry. So he resolved to cover the earth with water, and drown them. Only Condor and his sister, Raccoon, were saved, because Raccoon wove a basket to carry them on the waters. The new race that peopled the earth after the flood was descended from them.

Often the creators of the new world are depicted as riding on or materializing from the floodwaters. The Achomawi say a cloud formed on the waters, and that was Coyote, and then a fog, and that was Silver Fox. They became persons and floated in a canoe for years before Silver Fox formed the earth from the combings of his hair.

The Juaneño and Luiseño say that in the beginning there was nothing at all, just empty space.

Edward S. Curtis
Dancer with Deer Effigy
Hupa 1923

Hupa rituals celebrated the release of deer and salmon by the god Yimantuwingyai (He Who Is Lost to Us Across the Ocean) in the creation time. The Deerskin Dance of the Hupa was a ceremony that served the ritual purpose of renewing the world and the social purpose of displaying wealth. A male dancer might wear, for instance, a luxurious apron of civet skins; women's deerskin dance skirts were richly decorated with beading and hung with little brass bells. It was also known as the "along the river" dance, because the dancers moved upstream by canoe every day for ten days, dancing every afternoon and evening. Dancers carried deer effigies aloft on poles. The performance reminded old people of the dead who had formerly witnessed it with them, and caused them to weep.

And in that empty space, two clouds formed. One was called Vacant, and the other was called Empty. They were brother and sister.

She said, "I shall stretch myself out as big as I can. I shall shake and cause earthquakes. I shall roll around and around." And she became the Earth.

He said, "I shall rise up high and arch over everything. I shall cause men to die and take their souls up to the world above." And he became the Sky.

From this brother and sister everything which is to be found in this world was born.

These first deities, Vacant and Empty, are so abstract and remote as to be little more than poetic ideas. The god who instructed the people in their sacred ceremonies, taught them how to live, and promised that at death they should go to live with him among the stars, was much more personal. His name is Chungichnish, and he is worshiped with the ritual drinking of *toloache*, made from the hallucinogenic jimsonweed. It is in *toloache*-induced visions that boys being initiated into manhood dream of the animal who will be their sacred guide and helper through life.

Complex mythologies about the creation time were recorded from some of the Californian nations. For instance, the Wintu constructed a rich mythology about Olelbis ("One Who Is High Above"), who lived at the top of the sky, and his consort Mem Loimis ("Water Woman"), and the Achomawi built a whole cosmology around World's Heart, who lived in the center of the world.

The idea of dual creators, one high-minded and the other cunning and mischievous, is common. The Maidu, for instance, tell how the world was made by Earthmaker and Coyote. Earthmaker wanted to make the world perfect, but Coyote thwarted him at every turn.

Edward S. Curtis
Female Shaman
Hupa 1923

The Hupa believed sickness was caused either by the breaking of some magical observance or by the malevolence of some evil man with magical power. Most shaman doctors were women. They could diagnose illness by means of clairvoyance or dreams, or suck "pains" directly from the body, capturing the pains in basketwork cups. There was a special curing rite for children known as the Brush Dance, the aim of which was to persuade the people of the underworld to "give back" the soul of the sick child.

Earthmaker told the people, "If you see Coyote, kill him. He's bad all through."

The people went in search of Coyote, and at last they cornered him on a tiny, bare island. They kept him trapped there, so that he would starve to death. Earthmaker told them, "If after four days you hear no howling, then Coyote will be dead."

But Coyote dissolved himself into mist and drifted away across the water to land. Then he howled to

make the people's hair stand on end. So they knew that Coyote was not dead.

Every time the people tried to kill him, Coyote escaped.

So Earthmaker told them to make a big canoe and get in it, and then he flooded the world.

But at the last minute, Coyote slipped into the canoe, in disguise.

When the people came at last to land, where the peak of Canoe Mountain just poked out of the water, Coyote leaped first from the canoe and claimed the land for himself.

"Brother," said Earthmaker, "you are too powerful for me to kill. You have won."

And Coyote is still alive, causing trouble wherever he goes.

Stories of a great flood that destroyed life on earth, leaving only a small remnant to start again, are known all over North America. In California, people also tell of a great fire that caused a similar destruction.

The Wintu say this fire was caused by Loon Woman, who fell in love with her own brother when she found one of his hairs floating on the surface of a pool. Her brother ran away in horror, leaving a rotten log in his place. He and the rest of Loon Woman's family tried to flee to the sky in a basket. As it rose, they warned each other not to look down, or the basket would fall.

When Loon Woman got home to find them gone, she was so angry that she set fire to the lodge—and thus to the world. Coyote, who was in the basket, heard the fire crackling and wondered what was going on. Unable to resist, he peeked over the edge of the basket, sending it tumbling down into the flames. The whole family was burned to death, and Loon Woman made herself a necklace of their blackened hearts, which can still be seen as a black line around the neck of the common loon.

According to the Lake Miwok Indians, it was Snipe who set the world alight when White Goose Girl would not marry him. Like Loon Woman, he felt so angry and humiliated at the rejection of his love that he wanted to destroy the whole world. When the fire was raging, Snipe tried to fly to safety in the sky, but the flames licked ever higher, and burned him just as he reached the gate to the upper world.

The Maidu have a myth of how the First People stole fire from Thunder.

> Once there was a family who lived all crowded together in a sweat lodge. One of them went out hunting and never came back.
>
> First one, then another, then another, then another went out to look for him. Every one of them was

Edward S. Curtis
Basketry Designs
Yokuts 1924

While the Californian Indians are not much known for pottery, they were renowned basketmakers. These Yokuts baskets were woven from grasses and roots whose colors enabled various patterns to be made— for black, for instance, fern root was used. The designs were based on a few dozen basic elements, often representing such things as arrow points, snake markings, or deer feet. One Yokuts myth tells how, in the creation time, a girl who left home to seek her mother marked her trail with baskets featuring traditional patterns such as the gopher-snake design, the mountain design, and the rattlesnake design; her grandmother gathered them up, and so the people found out how to put designs on their baskets.

A. W. Chase
*Auburn, a Nisenan
Youth*
Nisenan c. 1870

*This young man is
splendidly arrayed in a
feathered headdress
with a gorget and sash
of abalone, all marks of
wealth. The Nisenan
Thunder myth tells of a
man who could not eat
the food of the earth,
only the food of the sky.
When he wanted to eat,
he would call out in
spirit language, and
acorn bread would
appear for him.
However much bread he
called for, there was no
end to it. One day his
grandsons spied on him
while he ate. He asked
them not to touch his
food, but they did, and
then it lost its magic
and would no longer
replenish itself. The man
sent the boys up into the
sky, and the thunder is
the sound of them
playing with their hoop,
rolling it back and
forth.*

stopped by a stranger, who challenged him to wrestle and then killed him and cut him up into pieces. It was the Great Green Lizard who did this terrible thing.

At last there was no one left but a sister and brother, a little boy with big eyes. And the boy said, "I'm going hunting."

His sister said, "Don't go. There are dangerous creatures out there. You won't be safe."

But he replied, "I am just as dangerous as they are."

He went out along the ridge until he came to the place where the others had been killed; their bones were lying all around.

Then the stranger, the Great Green Lizard, came up to him, and said, "Let's wrestle."

"All right," said the boy.

So they wrestled, and the boy killed the Great Green Lizard.

Then he went home and told his sister, "I am going up into the sky, into the meadows above. And when I get there, I shall call for you, so loudly the world will rumble."

When he got to the meadows above, he called out, and the whole world rumbled. But his sister did not go to him; she stayed where she was. All that spring he circled round the sky, rumbling, but she did not come.

At last he stopped, and the world fell silent. But when the next spring came, he started up again, rumbling, rumbling.

He was Thunder.

His cousin, Mosquito, came to stay with him. Thunder was hungry. He said, "Where can we find something to kill and eat?"

"We'll just have to look around," said Mosquito.

So Thunder rumbled all over the place, and the rain fell and the grass grew, but he couldn't find anything to kill and eat.

Mosquito knew where the people were living, and he went down and sucked their blood. But he didn't tell Thunder; he didn't want to share his food.

Winter came, and Thunder grew cold as well as hungry.

"There must be some people living down below," he said. "If they have fire, we could steal it and keep ourselves warm."

"No, no, that wouldn't be right," said Mosquito. He didn't want Thunder to find out where the people were living.

But Thunder said they should move down to the world below, where the food was, so they left the meadows above and built a lodge on West Mountain.

Eventually, Thunder made Mosquito promise to tell him where he was getting his food. But still Mosquito didn't want to say. Thunder might kill all the people, and Mosquito needed them alive, so he could suck their blood. So he told Thunder, "I get my food from trees. I don't kill many of them—just enough to get by. You could try eating a tree, if you're as desperate as all that."

The next day when Mosquito was out sucking blood from people, he heard the most tremendous crashing and banging in the air. He went back up to the lodge, and soon Thunder came home.

"I did it!" Thunder shouted.

Mosquito looked out, and on the mountainside there was a clump of trees, all smashed to the ground.

"You should only kill one of those tree people at a time," he said.

"Oh!" said Thunder.

Thunder went out looking for a lodge where people were living, and this time he found one. He went in gently, gently, not rumbling at all, and stole their fire. And then he threw it at a tree, striking the tree down with a lightning bolt. He laughed. "That will teach you to just stand around doing nothing," he said.

When he got back to West Mountain, he was still laughing. But when Mosquito heard he had stolen the fire from people, he was angry. He thought they might all die. And then what would he eat? So he packed up his things, moved out of Thunder's lodge, and went to live under a bush—and that's where mosquitoes have lived ever since.

Thunder didn't care. He went all over the land,

from lodge to lodge, stealing fire from people. Every time he saw the smoke of a fire, down he came and stole it, until he had stolen all the fire there was. He took it home and kept himself warm with it, as warm as could be.

He asked Nighthawk to keep an eye on it for him.

"I won't sleep," said Nighthawk. "I never sleep."

And Thunder gave him a necklace to pay him for sitting on the roof of the lodge, by the smokehole, guarding the fire.

The people didn't know what to do. They had killed a deer, but they had no fire to cook it on. They asked Magpie to come and glare at the raw meat. He stared and stared, and eventually the meat began to sear. But when they ate it, it was only cooked on the outside, not in the middle.

Every day the people looked over the land, hoping to see the smoke from a fire. And at last they did see smoke, coming from West Mountain. It was blowing from the smokehole of Thunder's lodge.

They went to investigate: Deer, Jackrabbit, Dog, Snake, Skunk with his flute—all the First People. But they were too big and noisy to sneak into Thunder's lodge without being caught. They didn't know what to do.

Then Mouse said to Skunk, "Will you lend me your flute?"

"Yes," said Skunk.

Mouse took the flute and crept into the lodge.

Nighthawk was still sitting on the roof by the smokehole. His eyes were closed, but he wasn't asleep. "I never sleep," he was saying. "No, not me. I'm always wide awake. . . . Wide awake."

Mouse crept up and stole the necklace from around Nighthawk's neck. Nighthawk didn't open his eyes, he just kept mumbling, "I never sleep. No, not me."

Then Mouse slipped down the smokehole and into Thunder's lodge. Thunder's daughters were sleeping in there, all snoring away. What if they wake up? thought Mouse. I wouldn't stand a chance. So Mouse nibbled away at the fastenings of their bark skirts. Then he stole some fire, put it safely inside Skunk's flute, and crawled back out the smoke hole.

When he got out, he gave some of the fire to Deer and some to Dog, and the three of them ran away.

The noise they made woke Thunder's daughters. They leaped up...and their skirts fell down. They had to stop to make themselves decent.

Deer, Dog, and Mouse ran as fast as they could.

Then Thunder's daughters stormed after them across the sky.

Deer couldn't run fast enough. He threw away the fire he was carrying into a cedar tree. Dog couldn't run fast enough. He threw away the fire he was carrying into an elderberry tree. Mouse couldn't run fast enough. He threw away the fire he was carrying into a buckeye tree.

All this time Thunder's daughters were like a cloud-burst at their heels.

Skunk was spraying them and Snake was biting

them—but that didn't stop Thunder's daughters from putting out all the fire.

Then they went home, and the sky cleared.

The people still didn't have any fire.

When Thunder got back to his lodge, he said, "It's not safe here. I shall take the rest of the fire up to the meadows above, where people can't come and steal it." And that's what he did. He doesn't live in this world anymore, but you can still hear him rumbling as he travels about in the meadows above.

After he was gone, the people wondered what to do.

"I know," said Mouse, and he went and fetched some buckeye wood.

Deer and Dog understood at once, and they went and fetched some cedar wood and some elderwood.

The people chopped up the elderwood and made fire starters from the cedar and the buckeye, and they made fire.

The people had fire, and it was stolen from them. They stole it back, and then they threw it away. And by throwing it away, they kept it forever.

That's how it happened, long ago, so they say.

The many comic touches in this myth may reflect the nature of the storyteller from whom it was recorded, Tom Young (Hánc'ibyjim), who is remembered as the last great Maidu storyteller. But the broad comedy in the myth is typical of Native American storytelling. The willingness to laugh at life is the balancing principle that keeps the Native American reverence for nature from becoming sanctimonious. The world is both sacred and profane—the creation of both Earthmaker and Coyote.

It was Coyote, say the Yokuts, who decided that people should not live forever. He said it out of pique, because he wanted human beings to have paws like his, and Lizard insisted that they should have hands with five fingers, like his. "Well, then," said Coyote, "they will have to die."

The Digueño, who live in the far south of California, have a different explanation of the origin of death.

> Long ago, when the moon had dwindled small, the people were running races, trying to keep up with the moon. When everyone had had their fun, Frog challenged Rabbit to a race. Everyone laughed, because Frog was such a funny shape.
>
> Frog was angry, and he shook his fists at the Maker, and said, "I shall make you pay for this."
>
> Now, the Maker, Tu-chai-pai, had retired to a high place to sleep. He didn't hear what Frog said. But next morning, when the sun rose, the Maker rose with it. He carried a long stick pointed at both ends. When he heard Frog muttering and swearing, he touched him with the stick, leaving a long white mark down his back.
>
> This made Frog even angrier. He went to the pool where the Maker drank and spat poison into the water.
>
> The Maker did not drink from the pool. As soon as Frog had done this evil thing, the Maker said to himself, "I shall die."
>
> He told the people, "I shall die with the moon." And when the moon had dwindled small once again, the Maker finished his life. He became six stars.
>
> And ever since then, every creature on earth must die, when the moon is right, for we are all children of Tu-chai-pai, the Maker.

Even the world will come to an end. The Wintu say that the world will last just as long as the Indians live. The Wintu shaman Kate Luckie said, "When the Indians all die, then God will let the water come down from the north. Everyone will drown."

But perhaps the end will just be a new beginning. For the world has, according to the Wintu, already been destroyed and remade four times before now.

Edward S. Curtis
Old Woman
Diegueño 1924

The Diegueño, like other tribes of southern California, observed a great annual mourning rite for the dead, at which goods and valuables were burned to supply the dead. Stuffed wildcat skins dressed in valuable dance regalia and made to look as human as possible were set up on stakes and "fed" during the mourning, then walked toward the fire and cast into the flames. These images were regarded as actually containing the ghost or spirit of the dead person.

93

7 THE GREAT BASIN AND PLATEAU

The Columbia Plateau, dominated by the great Columbia and Fraser Rivers, is home to a number of Salishan- and Sahaptin-speaking nations. Their culture was based on catching salmon, not hunting buffalo. The peoples of the Great Basin, which lies south of the Plateau and east of the Plains, were hunter-gatherers, adept at surviving in their arid homelands.

In Plateau culture there is a strong sense of the wonder of life. Every morning the Nez Perce would be awakened by a man known as the Herald of Dawn, who rode through the village, crying:

> I wonder if everyone is up! It is morning. We are alive, so thanks be! Rise up! Look about! Go see to the horses, lest a wolf has killed one! Thanks be that the children are alive!—and you, older men! and you, older women!—also that your friends are perhaps alive in other camps.

This celebration of life was tied to a deep reverence for the landscape in which the Plateau Indians lived. The great Nez Perce leader Chief Joseph movingly remembered his father's last moments.

> I saw he was dying. I took his hand in mine. He said, "My son, my body is returning to my mother earth, and my spirit is going very soon to see the Great Spirit Chief. When I am gone, think of your country. You are the chief of these people. They look to you to guide them. Always remember that your father never sold his country. You must stop your ears when you are asked to sign a treaty selling your home. A few years more, and white men will be all around you. They have their eyes on this land. My son, never forget my

Edward S. Curtis
The Guardian
Wishram 1910

This eerie face, carved on a large block of volcanic rock, represents a creation-time woman named Tsagiglálal, who long ago, before Coyote came up the river and changed things, was chief of all those who dwelled in the region. One of the things Coyote decreed was that women should no longer be chiefs, so he turned her into a rock, telling her to "stay here and watch over the people who will live at this place." The Wishram know that the Woman of the Rock sees all things, for whenever they look up at her, her large eyes are watching them. People made offerings to her in return for health, long life, or wealth, and women especially asked her help in matters of love and fertility.

95

dying words. This country holds your father's body. Never sell the bones of your father and mother." I pressed my father's hand and told him I would protect his grave with my life. My father smiled and passed away to the spirit land.

"I buried him in that beautiful valley of winding waters," Chief Joseph wrote. "I love that land more than all the rest of the world." Even so the Nez Perce were driven from their land.

This deep belief that the land was made for the people and the people for the land is central to Native American mythology. The Okanogon creation story tells how Old One made the earth out of a woman: "The soil is her flesh; the trees and vegetables are her hair; the rocks, her bones; and the wind is her breath."

The Yakima say that in the beginning the Great Chief Above lived in the sky all alone. Beneath him all was water. He went down and scooped up mud from below the water to create the land. He made the trees, the roots, and the berries. And then he made a man from a ball of mud and taught him to take the fish from the waters and the game from the forests. When the man became lonely, the Great Chief Above made a woman to be his companion and taught her how to dress skins, gather bark, roots, and berries, and cook the salmon and game that the man caught.

As in other culture areas, the creation is often seen as the dual responsibility of two brothers. One myth of the Owens Valley Paiute tells how Fish Eater and Hawk created the earth by shaking dirt from a rattle while they sang the world into being. But even among the Paiute, the more usual duo are Coyote and Wolf. In one myth, Coyote and Wolf create human beings by putting seeds into a jug and pouring them out as human beings.

The Lillooet tell how Mink and Coyote were helped in

the creation time by the Atseemath, which means "trans-formers." These beings had the ability to change one thing into another, so they were useful in putting the world in order. But they were mischievous troublemakers, and even when they were killed, they came back to life again.

The ability to transform himself is also Coyote's chief characteristic, and Coyote is the hero of myth after myth. He is so central to the mythic landscape that even myths that do not feature him are sometimes referred to as Coyote tales. And as in other culture areas, Coyote is essentially the playful aspect of the creator.

A Coeur d'Alene myth tells how Coyote was chosen by the first people to be the moon, and how they regretted their choice when he used his privileged position to spy on them and tell their secrets. They also say that Coyote once killed the Sun, in a fit of temper, and cut out his heart, leaving the world in darkness. Coyote tried to carry the Sun's heart home but kept falling over. Giving up, he threw it back into the sky, where it still shines today.

In the arid heat of the Great Basin, the Shoshone and the Paiute say that it was Cottontail who killed the Sun, throwing the Sun's gall bladder high into the sky. The reason he did this was to reduce the heat of the sun and to make the day last longer, to give himself more time to hunt rabbits.

The moon has a key role in the Coast Salish creation. Moon's story starts like that of the Star Husband folktale, known to many Indian nations. Two girls lie looking at the night sky and decide that they want to marry stars. They get their wish, but one gets a young handsome star, the other an old white-haired one.

In the sky world they spend their time as they did on earth, digging fern roots. Digging too deep, they make a

hole in the sky and escape back to earth through it. The girl with the young star husband gives birth to a baby, who is then stolen from her. He will grow to be the transformer, who returns as an adult, bringing all the knowledge and things that humans will need to live happily on earth.

A Nez Perce myth tells how Beaver brought this world the gift of fire. Sometimes he is said to have stolen it from the upper world. The people below were always cold, and when they saw lightning flashing in the sky, they wondered how they could get hold of this fire. The animals held a council, and Beaver was sent up to steal a spark from the Fire People, hiding it in his claw. A simpler version, set in Idaho, tells how Beaver won fire from the pine trees.

Before there were people in the world, the animals and the trees moved about and talked just as men do now.

Only the pine trees had the gift of fire. But no matter how cold it was, the pines would never let anyone else share the fire. They just huddled together, keeping warm, while everyone else shivered.

One winter it was so cold the animals and trees thought they would all freeze to death.

Beaver swam up the Grande Ronde River to where the pine trees were holding a council, and hid under the overhanging bank. The pine trees went for a swim in the river, but they never noticed Beaver. Then the pines built a large fire to warm themselves after bathing in the icy river.

Before long, a burning ember rolled out of the fire and into the river. Beaver caught it as it fell, tucked it in his breast, and swam away as fast as he could.

The pines ran after him, but they couldn't catch him. Whenever they caught up with him, he dodged from side to side of the river, and when he had shaken them off, he swam straight ahead. That is why to this day the Grande Ronde River twists and turns

Edward S. Curtis
Dusty Dress
Kalispel 1910

The shells sewn on this young Kalispel woman's dress imitate elk tusks. Her braids of hair are wound round with otter fur, and a weasel skin dangles from each. The marks on her hair were made with white clay; they probably denote her unmarried status. When coming into womanhood, a Kalispel girl was sent by her grandmother into the hills, where she fasted for six or eight days, all the while offering prayers to the objects she passed. To an old stump she would say, "I pray that I may become as old as you are!" To a large tree she would pray "that I may become as strong as you are!" After this she was called a woman and was ready to be married.

99

in some stretches and is perfectly straight in others.

At last the pines grew tired. Most of them stopped to rest on the riverbank, and they are still there today, in such a mass that hunters can hardly get through them. A few pines kept chasing Beaver, but they all gave up in the end, and they are scattered at intervals along the river, at the places where they stopped.

There was one cedar running at the head of the pines, and he said to the last few, "I'll go to the top of this hill and see how far ahead he is." So he ran to the top of the hill and saw Beaver just slipping into the Big Snake River, where the Grande Ronde enters it. So he knew that Beaver had got away.

The cedar could only watch helplessly as Beaver gave fire to the willows, and the birches, and other trees. Since then, all these trees have had fire in them, which can be lit by rubbing two pieces of wood together in the ancient way.

The cedar stood rooted to the spot, and he is still there today, although he is very old, so old that his top is dead.

That the chase was a very long one is shown by the fact that there are no other cedars for a hundred miles upstream of him. The old people point him out to the children. "Look," they say, "there is Old Cedar, still standing just where he stopped when he was chasing Beaver."

A widespread Plateau myth, told by Coeur d'Alene, Nez Perce, and Columbia River Indians, tells of the struggle between the Cold Weather Brothers and the Warm Weather Brothers. As in the myth of Beaver stealing fire, one group lives in warmth and luxury while the other freezes and starves. In the Coeur d'Alene story, Heat and Cold are two brothers; Heat is handsome, but Cold is ugly. While Heat is away, Cold starts freezing human beings to death. When Heat hears about it, he returns and makes the weather so hot that it kills his brother. Eventually, Cold comes back to life, and the two brothers agree to live in harmony; but still, if one or the

other goes too far from home, the brother left behind can cause extremes of heat or cold.

According to a Nez Perce version, Coyote persuaded the five Cold Brothers to wrestle with the five Warm Brothers and cut their heads off. From that time there was nothing but cold weather, and the old couple and their daughter, who were the only Cold People left, were forced to give all the fish they caught to the Warm People. But the eldest Warm Brother had a wife, who went back to her own people when the brothers were killed. She gave birth to a son, and when he grew to manhood, he returned and, with Coyote's encouragement, challenged the Cold Brothers to wrestle, and cut off *their* heads. So now cold weather must always give way to warm.

Another myth basic to Plateau culture shows Coyote in a better light, recounting how he freed the trapped salmon. The rancher Lucullus McWhorter—whose unpublished collections have been edited by Clifford E. Trafzer—recorded a version of this myth from Owl Child, a Wishram, in 1916:

> The five Beaver sisters lived at Celilo Falls on the Columbia River and made a dam there that prevented the salmon from swimming into the upper waters.
>
> Coyote said, "This is bad. Fish should be free for all the people."
>
> Coyote sat and thought about the problem. He decided he must go and see the Beaver sisters. But if he went as a man, they would not let him near. So he turned himself into a baby and floated down the river in a woven basket, crying, *"Wah! Wah!"*

The five sisters rescued him from the river and took him home. Only the youngest sister thought there was something odd about him.

Every day the sisters went out to dig roots, leaving the baby in the lodge. The first thing Coyote did when he was left alone was make himself five wooden hats and five root-digging sticks. He had a lot of work to.

Then, day after day, Coyote put on the five wooden hats, and went out and dug away at the dam with the root-digging sticks. By the time the sisters came home, he was back in the lodge, gurgling like a baby, but every day a little bigger, a little stronger.

"How fast the baby is growing!" the sisters said. "He is getting stronger every day."

On the fifth day, Coyote was so near to destroying the dam that he didn't go home.

When the sisters returned, they cried, "Our baby is gone!"

"Yes," said the youngest. "He has nearly broken the dam."

The sisters ran to the river. The first sister hit Coyote on the head with a wooden club, and the first wooden hat broke. Then the second sister hit him, and then the third, and the fourth, and the fifth.

All this time, Coyote was digging hard. When the fifth hat broke, so did the dam. The water rushed out, and the fish swam upstream.

Coyote let out a yell of triumph. "*Ha-a-a-a-aha!* When the new people come, they will have fish to eat. You cannot keep the salmon for yourselves. Salmon must be free for all."

Coyote created fishing places and waterfalls in the rivers and made the laws of how to catch and eat salmon. A Sanpoil myth tells how Coyote caught the first salmon for Old Man and Old Woman and taught them how to care for the salmon. After it was cooked, it was necessary to remove the backbone and the back part of the head, then wrap it in a sacred bundle of marsh grasses and bury it somewhere where it could not be stepped on or stepped over. By showing the salmon this

Edward S. Curtis
Salmon Fishing
Wishram 1909

According to Wishram myth, all the salmon were hoarded by two women. They were freed by Coyote, who turned the women into swallows, who always come when fish are caught. When Coyote saw the white salmon with their mouths agape, he made the first salmon spear. He speared a fish, steamed it, and ate it, saying, "Thus shall you people get white salmon in this land." The barbs on the double-pointed salmon spear are attached to the shaft by strong cords, so that when a speared fish struggles to escape, the barbs detach from the prong and the fish is held just the way it would be by a hook and line.

respect, the Sanpoil would ensure that they always had plenty of salmon in their traps.

In 1915, George Meninock, a Yakima chief, defended his nation's traditional fishing rights and put into words his profound sense of the natural bond between the Yakima and their homeland and the sacred bond between man and salmon. "When we were created, we were given our ground to live on, and from that time these were our rights," he said. "My strength is from the fish; my blood is from the fish, from the roots and the berries. The fish and the game are the essence of my life."

Although his actions broke the spell of winter and freed the salmon, Coyote also caused mankind to lose a precious prize: immortality.

When Coyote's daughter died, he tried to kill himself so that he could accompany her to the land above. But because he was only "half-cooked," he could not stay there. After five days he was told he must return to this world. His daughter gave him a package wrapped in buckskin, with strict instructions not to unpack it or look around before he had crossed the last of the five mountains he must travel over.

The pack was small, but as Coyote went along, it got heavier and heavier. And when he was nearly at the top of the fifth mountain, Coyote began to hear whispering and laughing behind him. It seemed to be coming from the pack. It spooked him. He threw down the pack and turned around.

There behind him Coyote saw his daughter and many other people he had met in the land above. His daughter told him, "The pack was full of all these ghosts. If you had carried it as I told you, and had not looked round, we would all have come alive again, and in the future no one would have stayed dead for more than two or three days. But from now on once people die, they will never return."

Coyote was very sad. He cried for five days, and then he stopped. There was nothing he could do about it.

Yellow Wolf, a Nez Perce who told a version of this myth to Lucullus McWhorter in 1924, placed this story "about five generations back." The sense that immortality and rebirth were in humanity's grasp so recently explains the spectacular collision between myth and history known as the 1890 Ghost Dance religion.

This new religion originated in the Great Basin, and its prophet was a Paiute medicine man called Wovoka (also known as Jack Wilson). Wovoka, according to the ethnologist James Mooney, was "one of those born to see visions and hear still voices."

Wovoka was around thirty years old when, on January 1, 1889, during a solar eclipse, he fell into a trance. He

Edward S. Curtis
*George Meninock,
a Yakima Chief*
Yakima 1910

George Meninock was an eloquent defender of Yakima hunting and fishing rights. "God created this Indian country and it was like he spread out a big blanket," he said. The Yakima tell how the five Frog brothers accompanied Grizzly Bear down the Yakima River, preparing the way for the human beings who were about to arrive: "A people are coming, a new people." They stopped at various points to argue about how long the night should be. The Frogs thought it should be one night only, while the Grizzly Bear, who likes sleeping, argued that every night should last for ten years. But the Frogs' incessant singing wore the Grizzly Bear down, and at last he agreed, "All right! Let it be one night."

James Mooney
Ghost Dancers
Arapaho 1891

The Arapaho were among the most enthusiastic followers of Wovoka. The Ghost Dance was based on the traditional Round Dance of the Paiute. The dancers formed a circle, and danced around singing special songs and often fainting in ecstasy; in this trance state, they experienced a kind of death and rebirth in which they communicated with their ancestors in the otherworld. The simple, repetitive songs—full of grief and longing— heralded the approach of the new earth. One of the seated dancers here has a crow, the sacred bird of the Ghost Dance, painted on his back. As the messenger from the spirit world, the crow hears and knows everything, both on earth and in the shadow land.

was said to have died, to have talked with God, to have saved the world by preventing the moon from devouring the sun, and then to have come back to life.

God told Wovoka that people must not fight or steal, for they were all brothers. He gave Wovoka "the power to destroy this world and all the people in it and have it made over again."

If the Indians danced as Wovoka instructed them, soon a new world would roll in on a whirlwind from the west, covering the old, exhausted earth and sweeping the whites and their world into the east. All the Indians who had died would be reborn, and a new age of peace and plenty would begin.

Delegates from many Indian nations flocked to hear the words of this new prophet. Waving an eagle feather over his upturned sombrero, Wovoka invited them to look inside. Those who believed in him saw there the whole spirit world and their ancestors. Those who did not believe saw just an empty hat.

The Ghost Dance spread like wildfire across the Plains and was taken up with particular enthusiasm by the Arapaho and the Sioux. Although Wovoka's message was entirely peaceful, the whites interpreted the Ghost Dance as a war dance and a sign of trouble to come.

The new world was prophesied to arrive in the spring of 1891, when the grass was an inch high. The Indians were in a fever of anticipation; the whites were in an extremely nervous state. On December 28, 1890, a band of more than 300 Miniconjou Lakota under the leadership of Big Foot, who were in the process of surrendering to the U.S. military, were gunned down by the rapid-fire Hotchkiss guns of the Seventh Cavalry in a merciless slaughter that came to be called the Battle of Wounded Knee. Most of the Lakota were unarmed, and many were women and children.

The whites felt threatened by this new religion, because they could not understand it. It was born out of the Native Americans' fear that their culture and their world were being buried or shoveled aside by the new ways. The new world that was prophesied would restore the natural law of the creation time.

Wovoka was regarded as the true prophet of that new

world. He could, it was said, light his pipe from the sun and form icicles in his hand. The sun was addressed by the Paiutes as Our Father and regarded as the creator, Wolf. The god who gave Wovoka his power was Wolf, who had made the world for the Indians in the first place.

As Michael Hittman shows in his biography, Wovoka himself was identified both with the Rainmaker, a mysterious messiah figure from the Paiute creation myth, and with Wolf himself—Paiutes called him Tamme Naa'a, Our Father, the same term they used for the sun.

The Ghost Dance was a new expression of the oldest themes in Paiute myth. A generation before, in 1870, another Paiute prophet, Wodziwob, had proclaimed an earlier Ghost Dance. Like Wovoka, Wodziwob preached that dancing would bring back the dead and establish a new paradise of eternal life on earth.

When Wodziwob's promised paradise failed, so, too, did his belief. He visited the happy land of the dead one last time, only to find a spoiled world of empty shadows. There were no happy ancestors, dancing and laughing— only the Owl, the harbinger of death, blinking his blank stare.

In ,contrast, Wovoka never lost faith in his vision. When the silent-film actor Tim McCoy met Wovoka in 1924, "he still talked of the coming millennium, in which the Indians would be given a new earth to dwell upon." Sitting in the back of the limousine that would take him home to the Yerington Indian Colony, Wovoka rolled down the window, dropped a cake of sacred red paint from Mount Grant, the place of the Paiute creation, into McCoy's pocket, and whispered, "I shall never die."

Anonymous
Wovoka with Tim McCoy
Paiute 1924

The name Wovoka translates as "The Woodcutter." It was while cutting wood in the mountains, during a solar eclipse on January 1, 1889, that Wovoka heard a great noise from above. According to one of his followers, "He laid down his ax and started to go in the direction of the noise, when he fell down dead; and God came and took him to heaven and showed him everything there. . . . Then God brought him back and laid him down where he had taken him from." Wovoka said that God had given him the power to destroy and remake the world by means of the Ghost Dance. When he met the actor Tim McCoy in 1924, Wovoka described how God told him he was the Messiah, on the day "when both he and the sun died."

8 THE NORTHWEST

The Native Americans of the Northwest Coast built up a rich culture based on fishing and hunting. Relatively wealthy and comfortable, they celebrated their surplus wealth by distributing it in giveaway feasts known as potlatch festivals. And yet the chief figure in their myths, Raven, is depicted as always hungry—he has another mouth in his stomach that can never be satisfied.

Stories and songs were a kind of wealth and were regarded as belonging to particular individuals or families. The complex structure of family and clan is at the heart of Northwest culture and Northwest myth. Someone traveling to a strange village had only to look at the carving on the totem poles to see which families shared his clan totem—Bear, Salmon, Beaver, Killer Whale, Raven—and therefore where he could expect a welcome, food, and shelter.

Totem poles are expressions of family pride, boasting of the family's lineage right back to the creation time, when animals could transform themselves into people and the totem animals carved on the poles founded the first families. A Raven totem pole may, for instance, show Raven holding the moon in his beak, stealing Beaver's lake, or releasing the salmon—all references to well-known myths. Among the Bella Coola, the stories that tell of the founding animal-ancestors were said to be stored in the House of Myths, above the sky.

The totem pole is not, as early observers thought, an idol to be worshiped; it is more like a family crest. But that does not mean that the totem pole has no mythic significance. It does—it represents the world tree, "the

Edward S. Curtis
A Nakoaktok Chief's Daughter
Kwakiutl 1914

The Nakoaktok are a Kwakiutl tribe. When the chief holds a potlach ceremony, at which he distributes property among the people, his eldest daughter sits enthroned above the guests, supported by carvings representing her slaves. The display of generosity in such a giveaway feast was a means of acquiring power and status; the more that was given away, the greater the respect that was earned. Both the custom of the potlatch and the practice of slavery reflect the surplus wealth that the Northwest Coast tribes were able to amass.

James G. Swan
*The Kwakiutl Village
at Alert Bay*
Kwakiutl 1879–80

*The Kwakiutl village is
shown here as it was
during the childhood of
Charles James Nowell,
Stranded Whale, who
told the story of
Wakiash and the first
totem pole and also
recorded his fascinating
life story in the book*
Smoke from Their Fires.
*The paintings on the
house front show a tally
of coppers, boats, and
blankets given away at
potlatches. The structure
to the left is the lookout
cage from which the
chief called out the
names of those receiving
gifts at the potlatch
ceremony.*

pole that holds up the sky," as the Kwakiutl myth of Wakiash shows.

There was once a chief named Wakiash, and he was named after the river Wakiash, because he was open-handed, flowing with gifts just as the river flowed with fish.

One time the tribe was having a big dance. All the other chiefs had dances that belonged to them, which they shared with the people. But Wakiash had never had a dance. He was unhappy about this. *I wish I had a dance*, he thought. So he decided to go up into the mountains to fast and think.

He stayed there for four days, fasting and bathing. On the fourth day he was so tired that he lay on his back and slept, and when he began to wake, he could feel a weight on his chest.

He heard a voice saying, "Wake up, so you can see where you are going!"

Wakiash opened his eyes and saw there was a little green frog sitting on his breast.

"Lie still," said the frog. "You are on the back of a raven, and it is going to fly around the world so that you may see what you want, and take it. I will come with you and stay with you until we come back to this place."

The raven took off and carried Wakiash and the frog all around the earth, showing him all the things of the world. They flew for four days, and when they were on their way back, Wakiash saw a house with a beautiful carved pole in front. He could hear the noise of singing and dancing and laughter coming from inside.

"These are fine things," said Wakiash. "I would like to take them with me."

The frog told the raven to land. "Hide behind the door," the frog told Wakiash.

The people in the room had stopped singing and dancing. They were uneasy. "There must be someone spying on us," they said. Although they were all animals, they had taken off their animal skins and looked just like people.

The beaver was the chief. He said, "Let one of us

112

who can run faster than the flames of the fire go
around the house and see."

The mouse said she would look. "I can get into anything, even a box, so if anyone is hiding, I can find
him." The mouse looked just like a woman.

She ran out, and Wakiash caught hold of her. "I am
your friend," he said. "Let me give you a gift." And he
gave her a piece of mountain goat's fat. The mouse
was so pleased with this that she asked Wakiash if
there was anything he wanted. "I want that carved
pole, and the songs and dances that go with it," he
said.

"Wait here," said the mouse.

The mouse went back in and said to the people,

"There's nobody outside." But when they tried to dance, they couldn't. They felt someone was watching. So they sent the mouse out again. Three times they did this, and each time the mouse spoke with Wakiash, telling him to wait. But the third time, she added, "When the dance begins, leap into the room."

When the mouse went back into the room and told the people that there was really no one watching, they started to dance. Then Wakiash sprang into the room, and they stopped dead. They were ashamed to be caught dancing in human shape, without their animal skins.

The mouse spoke up, saying, "Let's ask our friend here what he wants. He must want something, or he would not have come here."

"I would like this house, and that carved pole outside, and a dance of my own to go with it," said Wakiash.

"Sit down then and watch us dance," said the chief. "When we have finished, you can choose the dance you like best."

Wakiash watched. When the people finished dancing, the chief asked him which dance he liked best, and Wakiash chose the dance with the mask of Echo, who repeats all the noises he hears through different mouthpieces, and also the mask of the Little Man, who goes about the house talking, talking, and trying to pick a quarrel.

The chief was pleased with this and told Wakiash that he might take as many dances and as many masks as he liked, and also the house and the carved pole, which was called the sky pole, because it was so tall. The chief took the house and the sky pole and folded them into a little bundle. He tucked it into the Echo mask and said, "When you reach home, throw down this bundle, and the house will become as it was. Then you can give a dance."

Wakiash went back to the raven, and the raven flew away with him toward the mountain from which they had set out. On the way, Wakiash fell asleep. When he awoke, he was alone on the mountainside, and the raven and the frog were gone. But he still had the bundle, and he began to carry it home.

When he got home, he threw down the bundle, and it unfolded and turned back into a house. The whale painted on the house was blowing, the animals carved on the pole were making their noises, and all the masks inside the house were talking and crying aloud.

All Wakiash's people came to see what was happening, and Wakiash found that instead of four days, he had been away for four years. Then they went into the house, and Wakiash taught the people the songs and dances. Wakiash danced, and the Echo came, and whoever made a noise, the Echo made the same. All

Edward S. Curtis
Forest Spirit
Kwakiutl 1914

This Koskimo dancer represents Nuhlimkilaka, a female forest spirit whose name means "bringer of confusion." It is her doing when a hunter becomes confused and loses his way in the forest. The dancer representing her plays a role in the núnhlim ceremony, a dance in which the young man of the house, supposedly abducted by some spirit, returns, magically revived, to general rejoicing.

115

Lloyd Winter and
Percy Pond
*Interior of the
Whale House*
Chilkat 1896

*Winter and Pond were
made members of the
Chilkat tribe when they
accidentally stumbled
across a secret potlach.
Being adopted into the
tribe enabled them to
capture this rare view of
the interior of the Whale
House at Klukwan, the
center of Chilkat ritual
life. The standing man
is Chief Coudawhot. The
design on his dancing
costume probably
represents a beaver—all
the designs and objects
have a mythical
meaning and a ritual
use. The elaborately
carved wooden
backdrop is called a
"rain screen."*

the chiefs agreed that Wakiash had the best dance of all.

When they had finished dancing, the house and all its contents disappeared. They went back to the animals.

So Wakiash made a new house out of wood, and new masks. And then he carved the first totem pole, to stand outside the house, and he called it Kalakuyuwish, the pole that holds up the sky. And when it creaked, the people said, "It is because the sky is so heavy."

This story contains many distinctive features of Northwest culture. It explains the origin not just of the totem pole but also of the ceremonial winter dances in which elaborately masked dancers imitate the animal-people of the creation time.

In the story of Wakiash, the raven is simply his mode of transport, and the frog his helper and adviser—but they are also Raven and Frog, two of the most powerful beings of the creation time.

Raven is the trickster-creator and the most important figure in Northwest Coast mythology. Some stories do mention a remote Lord of the Sky who first made the world; the Tsimshian say that when Walks All Over the Sky slept, sparks flew from his mouth and became the stars. But this first creator does not feature strongly in the myths and ceremonies of the Northwest; sometimes this is explained by a story telling how the sky world used to be nearer the earth than it is now, but the Lord of the Sky was irritated by the constant hulla-baloo from the people below and moved farther away.

Raven, on the other hand, always interests himself in human affairs—too much so for comfort sometimes! His name among the Haida means "the one who is going to order things," and putting the world in order was his first task. This involved transforming the things that first

existed into their current forms and establishing the laws of nature. In some Northwest cultures, such as the Salish and Wakashan tribes (which include the Kwakiutl), there was a separate myth cycle of a transformer who undertook these tasks. The Kwakiutl call him Kánikala and tell stories of his encounters with the clan ancestors celebrated on their totem poles.

One of the most complete cycles of stories about Raven was recorded by Henry W. Tate, a Tsimshian, for the ethnologist Franz Boas. It begins by telling how at the time when the world was still covered with darkness, a chief of the animal-people lost his son. The parents were so overcome with grief, wailing every morning over the boy's corpse, that they were sent a new child from the sky, "a youth, bright as fire." This was Raven.

At first his parents were worried because the child would not eat—but then the greedy slave Mouth at Each End fed Raven a scab from his shinbone, and he became voracious. He ate all the food of the tribe, and was still hungry. At last the chief had to send him away. He gave him a raven cloak and told him to fly over the land, scattering berries and fish roe, to make sure that he would never go hungry.

The second myth tells how Raven obtained light for the world.

After he had scattered the fruits over the land and the salmon roe and trout roe in the rivers, Raven began to worry about how he would gather his food if the world remained dark. The only light was the light from the stars, and even that could be covered up by clouds. He remembered that there was light up in the sky world, where he had come from. So he put on his raven cloak and flew up through a hole in the sky.

When Raven saw the daughter of the sky chief going to fetch water, he transformed himself into a leaf on the surface of the pool. When she dipped her bucket into the water, she scooped up the leaf, too, and when she drank some water, she swallowed the leaf.

Soon the sky chief's daughter gave birth to a baby boy. It was Raven again. She loved him and looked after him. He grew up quickly, but nothing seemed to make him happy. He just cried all the time.

Eventually, his mother worked out what was wrong. Raven was crying for the light that hung in a box in the corner of the house. He wanted to play with it. When she gave it to him, he stopped crying, and for four days he rolled it around inside the house. Sometimes he rolled it as far as the door, but the chief didn't think anything about it.

At last, when Raven had rolled the light to the door, he picked it up, put it on his shoulder, and ran away. The sky people ran after him, shouting, "He is stealing the light!" but they couldn't catch him. When he got to the hole in the sky, he put on his raven cloak and flew down to this world, carrying the light.

He landed at the mouth of a river. He could hear the people fishing out on the water. "Throw me a fish," he called. "I'm starving."

But the animal-people just laughed at him.

"I've brought you a light from the sky world," Raven said. "But if you don't give me a fish, I will break it."

"You liar!" they said.

He asked them four times, and four times they refused. So, in a temper, Raven smashed the box of light he had stolen from the sky.

And daylight spread throughout the world.

Raven's attempt to destroy the light only spreads it all over the world. Here, as elsewhere, his actions don't have quite the effect he wants. Later, for instance, he marries Bright Cloud Woman, a salmon-woman who just has to dip her fingers into water to create more salmon. When Raven makes himself a comb from a salmon's backbone (instead of returning it to the water, where it will become a new salmon), and then blames Bright Cloud Woman for the way it tugs at his hair, she leaves him and takes the salmon with her.

The story of Raven breaking open the sky chief's box of light explains why the world is not dark, but it does not mention the sun—who is probably to be identified with the sky chief himself, Raven's true father. A Bella Coola myth makes this connection clear, though this time the trickster figure is Mink, not Raven.

Once there was a woman of the Bella Coola who refused offers of marriage from all the young men of the tribe. "If I can't marry the Sun, I won't marry anyone," she said.

Finally, she left her village and went up to the sky to seek the Sun. She married him, and after she had been there one day, she had a child. He grew very quickly, and on the second day he was able to walk and talk.

The boy wanted to go down to earth and see his grandparents. Talking of them made his mother homesick, and she started to cry. Seeing how sad she was, the Sun said, "You may return to earth. Slide down my eyelashes." His eyelashes were the sunbeams, and he sent them right down into his wife's home.

Case and Draper
Kaa-Claa in Potlatch Dancing Costume
Tlingit 1906

This Tlingit woman is resplendent in her potlatch dancing costume, including an intricately embroidered dress, a nose ring, face paint, and a bear-claw headdress. The excessive consumption at a potlatch feast was in contrast with the hand-to-mouth existence led by Hayicanako, Old Woman Underneath Us, who supports the earth in Tlingit mythology. Sometimes she gets so hungry that she trembles, causing an earthquake; she can be satisfied by people throwing grease into their cooking fires.

So the Sun's wife and child stayed on earth, and the boy played with the other village children. One day they teased him, saying he didn't have a father. He began to cry and ran to his mother, begging her for a bow and arrows, and she gave them to him.

The first arrow he shot stuck in the sun. The second arrow stuck in the first arrow, and the third arrow stuck in the second, and so on until the boy had shot a chain of arrows from the earth up to the sky. Then he climbed up the arrows and entered the Sun's house.

He told his father how the boys had teased him and asked if he could carry the sun the next day. But his father said, "It would be too much for you. I have to carry a lot of torches—small ones to burn in the morning and afternoon, and big ones to burn at noon." But the boy insisted. So next morning the Sun allowed him to take the torches, telling him to be careful to burn them in the right order.

The boy set off across the sky, carrying all the torches. But he couldn't be bothered to light them one at a time. Instead, he lit them all at once.

It grew very hot. The trees began to burn, and all the animal-people jumped into the water to save themselves. But then the water began to boil.

The boy's mother spread out her blanket, and the animals hid under it and were saved. But some of the animals were scorched. The ermine hid in a hole, but the tip of its tail was sticking out, and is black to this day. The mountain goat hid in a cave, and so it is pure white, but all the animals that did not hide were burned black.

The Sun saw what was happening, and shouted, "Stop! If you carry on like that, there will be no people left on earth!"

The Sun took the torches back and cast the boy out of the sky, saying, "You shall be the mink, and men shall hunt you for all time."

Just as this naughty boy's father is the Sun, so his mother seems to be the Earth, able to spread out her blanket and save the animal-people from the world fire.

Mink is the trickster figure among the Bella Bella, Kwakiutl, Nootka, and Kathlamet. He is even more mischievous than Raven, because much of his role of preparing the world for humans is taken by the transformer, Kánikala, who is said to be Mink's older brother.

Another widespread myth of the Northwest Coast is that of Bear Mother. She is a haughty young girl who is offended when she steps in some bear dung. She makes angry remarks about the bears. In return, the bears capture her while she is out picking berries, and one of them makes her his wife. She gives birth to twin bear cubs.

The girl is tracked down and rescued by her brothers, who kill her bear husband—but not before he has passed his magical powers on to the bear cubs, enabling them to turn themselves into human beings and making them the greatest hunters ever known among their mother's people.

The first beings of the creation time were both animals and people, like these bear cubs, and it is from them that both the human beings and the animals of today are descended. The clan or family allegiance to a particular animal, carved in wood on a totem pole, is not just a matter of history or sentiment. It is a living link to the creation time, the past that is always present.

9 THE ARCTIC

The myths of the Inuit have a harsh, elemental poetry that reflects the unforgiving world in which they live. The chief figure is Raven, the creator, culture hero, and trickster, who came down from the sky world and made the earth when everything was covered in water.

In the nineteenth century, Edward William Nelson collected the following creation myth from an old Unalit man living at Kigiktauik on Norton Sound in Alaska. He had heard it when he was a boy from an old man who, when he had finished telling it, would pour a cup of water on the floor, saying, "Drink well, spirits of those of whom I have told."

It was in the time after Raven had made the earth. There were no people. But the first man was there, all coiled up in the pod of a beach pea.

For four days the man lay there. On the fifth day he stretched out his feet and burst the pod, falling to the ground, where he stood up, a grown man.

He looked about him and then moved his hands and arms, his neck and legs, and looked himself all over.

He started to walk and came to a pond. He stooped down to drink some water. It felt good.

Just then he saw something dark flapping toward him. It was a raven. It landed near him, and as it touched the ground, it pushed up its beak onto its forehead and turned into a man. It was Raven.

Raven stared at the man. "What are you?" he asked. "Where have you come from? I have never seen anything like you before."

"I came from the pea pod," said the man.

"Ah!" said Raven. "I made that plant, but I did not know that anything like you would ever come from it."

Soon the man became hungry. Raven pulled down his beak and turned back into a bird. He flew off and came back with four berries—two salmonberries and two heathberries. "I have made these for you to eat," he said.

The man ate them, and they were good.

Raven took the man to a small creek, and from the clay at the water's edge he molded a pair of sheep. Raven pulled down his mask and waved his wings over the images four times, and they came to life. Then he made two reindeer in the same way.

Then Raven looked at the man. "You will be lonely, all by yourself," he said. He took clay from a spot some distance from where he had made the animals, made an image much like the man, and fastened fine water grass to the back of the head for hair. After the image had dried, he waved his wings over it, and a beautiful young woman arose and stood beside the man. "She will be a companion for you," said Raven.

Raven made everything in the world and taught man how to live in it—how to make fire, how to make kayaks, how to catch seals, and so on. When it seemed that men might destroy everything he had made, he created the bear, to teach men fear. When it seemed that they might kill all the animals, he stole the sun, plunging the world into darkness to teach them a lesson.

One myth about Raven tells how he was once trapped inside a whale. It illustrates the Inuit belief that every living thing has a soul, or *inua*, which is the life force. It is Raven's strong *inua* that enables him to transform himself from bird to man and back again.

Raven flew far out to sea—so far that he grew tired. He looked for somewhere to rest, but there was no land. So he flew down the open mouth of a whale.

Inside the whale it was as neat as an igloo. On a bed sat a young woman, tending a glowing oil lamp. She was the whale's *inua*. She made Raven welcome and fed him berries.

Every time the whale rose to the surface to draw

Edward S. Curtis
Maskette
Nunivak 1928

The effect of this maskette worn on the forehead is very much as Raven is imagined when he has pushed his beak up and turned into a man. Such maskettes represent the spirit powers of their owners. This one shows a predatory bird with a fish caught in its mouth; a miniature spear is stuck in the top of the fish's head. It was painted blue, with the eyes, mouth, and nostrils of the bird outlined in red.

breath, she slipped out into the air and then back in again.

While she was out, Raven meddled with the oil lamp and snuffed out the flame. That oil lamp was the whale's heart, and when it went out, the whale died. The *inua* never came back, and Raven was left trapped in the body of the dead whale.

For four days Raven struggled in the blood and the dark, until at last he managed to haul himself out of the whale's mouth. He perched on the floating

carcass, too tired to fly—a naked raven, smeared with grease and filth, on the back of a dead whale.

A storm came and drove the whale toward land. The people came out in the kayaks to bring it in. When Raven saw them coming, he changed himself back into a man.

"I killed the whale! I killed the whale!" he crowed, and he became a great man among the people.

In his book *Ancient Land: Sacred Whale*, Tom Lowenstein shows how for the Tikigaq people of Alaska the myth of Raven and the whale lies at the heart of their culture. Tikigaq was the name of the very first whale, which was harpooned by Raven and turned into their land—Tikigaq, or Point Hope. "The land is alive," they say.

The Tikigaq igloo, with its whalebone entrance passage, represents the whale. When the Tikigaq men hunt whales, they enact the part of Raven, in raven-skin capes; when they catch a whale, they thrust a raven's head into the whale's mouth, "to feed it fresh meat." Meanwhile, the women remain in the igloo, passive, enacting the part of the whale's *inua*. The verb *ani* means both "to leave the igloo" and "to be born."

The whale hunt is not just a search for food, but a re-enactment of a sacred history.

In Alaska, they also tell an epic cycle of stories about the adventures of a transformer hero in the creation time, called Qayaq in the version written by the Inupiat storyteller Lela Kiana Oman, and Wander-Hawk in the earlier version recorded by Knud Rasmussen. This hero wanders across the landscape, fighting evil beings and transforming himself into all kinds of animals, birds, and fish in the course of his adventures. Eventually he returns home to his parents, only to discover that their house has wasted away, and a great tree grown in its place, but even that is now no more than a stump. Hundreds of years had past, and his parents were long gone. Qayak turned into a hawk and sat on the stump, his head bowed with grief.

The Inuit share with the other Native American hunting cultures the belief that the supply of game is controlled by a master or mistress of life. The master of the land animals is Moon Man, and the sea mammals are the gift of Sea Woman, who is often named Sedna.

The story of how Sedna became the mother of the sea beasts is cruel and unyielding in all its forms. Usually, she is made to suffer because she has chosen to marry an animal—often a dog but sometimes a sea bird such as a fulmar. But in the Netsilik version collected by Knud Rasmussen, she is persecuted just because she is an unwanted orphan girl.

Edward S. Curtis
Ready for the Throw
Nunivak 1928

Sealing was of prime importance to the Inuit of Nunivak Island; seals were hunted in spring and fall during their northward and southward migrations. The first seals were born from the severed fingers of the sea mother, Sedna. According to Inuit myth, the earth is surrounded by high mountains with only one entrance, through which the first people came. Later, travelers in a kayak tried to leave the same way, but the cliffs closed on them and broke off one end of their kayak. Ever since, kayaks have only had one pointed end.

Once, a long time ago, the people left their settlement to find new hunting places. They had to cross the water, so they made a raft of kayaks to get across. There wasn't enough room on the kayaks, and when they began to sink under the weight, the people pushed Sedna overboard. Nobody cared about her since she was just an orphan girl.

Sedna tried to grab hold of the edge of the raft, but they cut off her fingers, and she sank to the bottom of the sea.

Her severed fingers came to life, and they became the first seals.

Now she lives in her house at the bottom of the sea and is the mother of the sea beasts. She has great power over mankind. Whenever anyone breaks a taboo, Sedna knows. And then she shuts up all the sea beasts, and the people begin to starve.

Sedna can be placated only by a shaman who is brave enough to make the terrifying journey to her house under the sea, pass the fierce dog that guards her, and brush and braid her hair for her—for all the sins of humankind fall through the sea and collect as dirt in Sedna's hair, and without fingers she cannot brush it for herself.

The importance of the shamans in Inuit life was crucial, for it was they who traveled to the moon and to the bottom of the sea to plead for the release of the animals without which the people would starve. But although shamans were therefore in great regard, the children played a "spirit game" that both imitated and parodied shaman seances, with, as Knud Rasmussen put it, "a capital sense of humor."

Rasmussen was curious as to why the adults allowed such blasphemy and asked one Netsilik man if it was wise. The man answered, with astonishment all over his face, that "the spirits really understood a joke."

One Iglulik myth, however, tells of a group of children who overstepped the mark. Playing the spirit game, they called up a ferocious spirit who thrashed them, using a live bearded seal as a whip.

Not all spirits are so hostile to mankind. A myth told to Rasmussen by Sagluaq, from Colville River, tells how an eagle spirit gave mankind a great gift. It is the story of how joy came to man.

> Once upon a time, men and woman knew no joy. All they did was work, eat, and sleep. One day was just like another. They worked, they ate, they slept. Next day they rose and did it all again.
>
> There was a man and his wife and their three strong sons, who lived by the sea. Every day the sons went hunting and brought their catch home to their parents. They worked, they ate, they slept.
>
> But then disaster fell. First the eldest son and then

Edward S. Curtis
Ceremonial Mask
Nunivak 1928

In their festivals the Inuit wear wooden masks that, said one shaman, "are symbolic of the world and all the people. . . . They represent, in our festivals, only what people desire." The wearer is imbued with the spirit power of the mask. Male and female masks are similar, but the male ones have a mustache. Both have a humanlike face, with a hoop surround from which miniature wooden hands and feet and feathers project.

the middle one did not return from the hunt. Now only the youngest son was left, and without his skill at hunting, the man and his wife would starve. So every night they waited anxiously for him to come home.

One day the youngest son, whose name was Teriak, was stalking a caribou when an eagle began to circle above him. It flew right down to the ground, and when it landed, it turned into a young man in a gleaming cloak of eagle feathers. "What is the secret of life?" asked the eagle.

"The secret of life is to work, eat, and sleep," said Teriak.

"You are no better than your foolish brothers," said the eagle. "I killed them, and I will kill you, too, unless you show more sense. The secret of life is joy, and only when you have learned to sing and dance for joy will I let you return home."

So Teriak had to go with the eagle. They walked and walked until they came to a high mountain, and they started to climb. As they got higher, Teriak could hear a great rhythmic throbbing that echoed across the mountainside. "What is that noise?" he asked.

"That is the beating of my mother's heart," said the eagle.

When they reached the eagle's house, they found his mother, sitting all alone. Although her heart was beating so loud, she seemed old and feeble and sad.

The eagle said to her, "This is Teriak. I have brought him here to learn how to sing and dance for joy."

"First you must build a feast hall that is big enough for many men," said the mother.

"But we know of no men but ourselves," said Teriak.

"You are lonely because you have left no room in your lives for joy," said the old eagle. "Let joy in, and others will come."

And then she taught Teriak how to put words together and make a song, and how to fit those words to a tune. She taught him how to beat out a rhythm on a drum and how to dance.

"Now you are ready to return to your home," she said. "You have learned well."

"How can I repay you for this gift of joy?" asked Teriak.

"Teach others what I have taught you and hold a festival of song," replied the old eagle. "In that way you will repay me."

Then the eagle's son told Teriak to climb up on his back. Teriak clung around his neck, and the eagle launched himself off the mountainside into the cold, clear sky. They flew through the air until they reached the place where they had met, and there the eagle set Teriak safely down on the earth. "Farewell," he said. "Remember, when you hold a festival of song, you will repay all you owe."

When Teriak arrived home, he told his parents all that had happened. "So you see," he finished, "what has been lacking from our lives is joy. We must invite all men to a festival of song, so that I can teach them all how to share this wonderful gift."

Teriak's parents could not understand what he was

talking about. "Nothing is missing from life," they said. "Work, eat, sleep—that was good enough for our parents, and their parents before them, so it is good enough for us." But they were frightened that the eagle would come back and kill Teriak, leaving them to starve, so they agreed to hold the song festival.

They built a feast hall and filled it with good things to eat. And then Teriak taught his father and mother how to make songs. "Look through your memories," he said, "and find the most precious moments. Take them and polish them until they shine like the rays of the sun, and then sing them out on your breath. Let your thoughts break over you like a wave over the sea."

And so they were ready to hold the song festival. Teriak went out into the world to invite people to the festival, and he discovered that he and his parents were no longer alone. Everywhere he went, he met people. They were always in pairs and clad in animal skins. Some wore wolfskins, some the furs of the wolverine, the lynx, the red fox, or the silver fox—all the animals. Teriak invited them all to the festival.

Soon the feast hall was full of the sounds of laughter and merriment. Guest after guest danced and sang, and of all the songs the one that caused the most laughter and cheer was the one that Teriak sang, and it only had one word:

> Joy, joy,
> Joy, joy!

Teriak's heart beat in time to the drum. It seemed to him that his joy was booming out across the world.

And so the night passed, and it was dawn. As the first light came, the guests dropped down onto their hands, and sprang away on all fours—turned back into wolves, wolverines, lynxes, red foxes, silver foxes, and all kinds of animals that roam the land. For the power of joy is so strong that it can even turn animals into humans.

That day Teriak met the eagle once more. He climbed without fear onto the eagle's back and flew to the top of the mountain to meet the eagle's ancient mother and tell her about the song festival. But when he reached the eagle's home, he could not see the feeble old eagle anywhere. For the sound of joy rising up from the earth had made her young and strong again.

And so it is that men and women must always keep a light heart and share in the gift of joy, for the sounds of our merrymaking will make old eagles young again, and repay the eagle's gift.

Lomen Brothers
Wolf Dancers
Kaviagamute c.1900

The Wolf Dance of the Kaviagamute was meant to ward off wolves. The wolf is a symbol of ferocity in Alaskan Inuit myth. One Noatak story tells of man who was so irritated by his mother-in-law that he decided to become an animal. His first thought was to join a pack of wolves, but a wolf dissuaded him, saying, "You want to join us, but my friends say that when it is stormy and we have no food, we always eat another wolf. When we see a man hunting and we are short of food, we always eat him. Why don't you try to become some other kind of animal?" So the man became a caribou.

BIBLIOGRAPHY

GENERAL

Bierhorst, John. *The Mythology of North America*. New York: William Morrow, 1985.
———. *The Red Swan: Myths and Tales of the American Indians*. New York: Farrar, Straus and Giroux, 1976. Reprinted by the University of New Mexico Press, 1992.
Burland, Cottie. *North American Indian Mythology*. London: Paul Hamlyn, 1965.
Curtis, Edward S. *The North American Indian*. Vols. 1–5, Cambridge, Mass.: The University Press, 1907–09. Vols. 6–20, Norwood, Conn.: Plimpton Press, 1911–30.
Edmonds, Margot, and Ella E. Clark. *Voices of the Winds: Native American Legends*. New York: Facts On File, 1989.
Erdoes, Richard, and Alfonzo Ortiz. *American Indian Myths and Legends*. New York: Pantheon, 1984.
Gill, Sam D., and Irene F. Sullivan. *Dictionary of Native American Mythology*. New York and Oxford: Oxford University Press, 1992.
Leeming, David, and Jake Page. *The Mythology of Native North America*. Norman: University of Oklahoma Press, 1998.
Taylor, Colin. *Myths of the North American Indians*. London: Calman and King, 1995.
——— (ed.). *The Native Americans: The Indigenous People of North America*. London: Tiger Books International, 1995.
Thompson, Stith. *Tales of the North American Indians*. Cambridge, Mass.: Harvard University Press, 1929. Reprinted by Indiana University Press, 1966.

THE NORTHEAST

Bierhorst, John. *Mythology of the Lenape*. Tucson: University of Arizona Press, 1995.
Curtin, Jeremiah, and J. N. B. Hewitt. *Seneca Fiction, Legends and Myths*. Washington, D.C.: Smithonian Institution, Bureau of American Ethnology, 32nd Annual Report, 1918.
Hoffman, W. J. *The Mide'wiwin or "Grand Medicine Society" of the Ojibwa*. Washington, D.C.: Smithsonian Institution Bureau of American Ethnology, 7th Annual Report, 1891.
Leland, Charles G. *The Algonquin Legends of New England*. Boston: Houghton Mifflin, 1884. Reprinted as *Algonquin Legends* by Dover Books, 1992.
Parker, Arthur C. *Seneca Myths and Folk Tales*. New York: Buffalo Historical Society, 1923. Reprinted by the University of Nebraska Press, 1989.
Radin, Paul. *The Trickster: A Study in American Indian Mythology*. New York: Schocken Books, 1956.
Schoolcraft, Henry Rowe. *Schoolcraft's Indian Legends*. Edited by Mentor L. Williams. East Lansing: Michigan State University Press, 1956.
Skinner, Alanson, and John V. Satterlee. *Folklore of the Menomini Indians*. New York: Anthropological Papers of the American Museum of Natural History, no. 13, 1915.
Spindler, George, and Louise Spindler. *Dreamers with Power: The Menominee*. Prospect Heights, Ill.: Waveland Press, 1984.

THE SOUTHEAST

Dorsey, George A. *Traditions of the Caddo*. Washington, D.C.: Carnegie Institute of Washington, 1905. Reprinted by the University of Nebraska Press, 1997.

Lankford, George E. *Native American Legends: Southeastern Legends —Tales from the Natchez, Caddo, Biloxi, Chickasaw, and Other Nations*. Little Rock, Ark.: August House, 1987.

Mooney, James. *Myths of the Cherokee*. Washington, D.C.: Smithsonian Institution, Bureau of American Ethnology, 19th Annual Report, 1900. Reprinted by Dover Publications, 1995.

———, *The Swimmer Manuscript: Cherokee Sacred Formulas and Medicinal Prescriptions*. Edited by F. M. Olbrechts. Washington, D.C.: Smithsonian Institution, Bureau of American Ethnology, Bulletin 99, 1932.

Swanton, John R. *Myths and Tales of the Southeastern Indians*. Washington, D.C.: Smithsonian Institution, Bureau of American Ethnology, 1929. Reprinted by the University of Oklahoma Press, 1995.

———. *Religious Beliefs and Medical Practices of the Creek Indians*. Washington, D.C.: Smithsonian Institution, Bureau of American Ethnology, 42nd Annual Report, 1928.

Wagner, Günter. *Yuchi Tales*. Publications of the American Ethnological Society, vol. 13. New York: G. E. Stechert, 1931.

THE PLAINS

Beckwith, Martha Warren. *Mandan-Hidatsa Myths and Ceremonies*. New York: American Folklore Society, 1938.

Brown, Joseph Epes. *The Sacred Pipe: Black Elk's Account of the Seven Rites of the Oglala Sioux*. Norman and London: University of Oklahoma Press, 1953.

Catlin, George. *O-Kee-pa: A Religious Ceremony; and Other Customs of the Mandans*. Philadelphia: J. B. Lippincott, 1867.

Crow Dog, Leonard, and Richard Erdoes. *Crow Dog: Four Generations of Sioux Medicine Men*. New York: HarperCollins, 1995.

DeMallie, Raymond J., and Douglas R. Parks. *Sioux Indian Religion*. Norman and London: University of Oklahoma Press, 1987.

Dorsey, George A. *The Mythology of the Wichita*. Washington, D.C.: Carnegie Institute, 1904. Reprinted by the University of Oklahoma Press, 1995.

———. *The Pawnee: Mythology (Part 1)*. Washington, D.C.: Carnegie Institute, 1906. Reprinted as *The Pawnee Mythology* by the University of Nebraska Press, 1997.

Fletcher, Alice C., and Francis La Flesche. *The Omaha Tribe* (2 vols.). Washington, D.C.: Smithsonian Institution, Bureau of American Ethnology, 27th Annual Report, 1911. Reprinted by the University of Nebraska Press, 1992.

Grinnell, George Bird. *Blackfoot Lodge Tales*. New York: Charles Scribner's Sons, 1920. Reprinted by the University of Nebraska Press, 1962.

———. *Pawnee Hero Stories and Folk-Tales*. New York: Forrest and Stream Publishing Company, 1889. Reprinted by the University of Nebraska Press, 1961.

La Flesche, Francis. *The Osage and the Invisible World*. Edited by Garrick A. Bailey. Norman and London: University of Oklahoma Press, 1995.

Lowie, Robert H. *Myths and Traditions of the Crow Indians*. New York: American Museum of Natural History, 1918. Reprinted by the University of Nebraska Press, 1993.

Mails, Thomas E. *Fools Crow*. Garden City, N.Y.: Doubleday, 1979. Reprinted by the University of Nebraska Press, 1990.

Murie, James R. *Ceremonies of the Pawnee*. Edited by Douglas R. Parks. Washington, D.C.: Smithsonian Institution Press, 1981. Reprinted by the University of Nebraska Press, 1989.

Neihardt, John G. *Black Elk Speaks*. New York: Morrow, 1932. Reprinted by the University of Nebraska Press, 1979.

Parks, Douglas R. *Myths and Traditions of the Arikara Indians*. Lincoln and London: University of Nebraska Press, 1996.

Walker, James R. *Lakota Belief and Ritual*. Edited by Raymond J. DeMallie and Elaine A. Jahner. Lincoln and London: University of Nebraska Press, 1980.

———. *Lakota Myth*. Edited by Elaine A. Jahner. Lincoln and London: University of Nebraska Press, 1983.

Wissler, Clark, and D. C. Duvall. *Mythology of the Blackfoot Indians*. New York: American Museum of Natural History, 1908. Reprinted by the University of Nebraska Press, 1995.

THE SOUTHWEST

Bahr, Donald, et. al. *The Short Swift Time of Gods on Earth: The Hohokam Chronicles*. Berkeley, Los Angeles, London: University of California Press, 1994.

Benedict, Ruth. *Zuñi Mythology* (2 vols.). New York: Columbia University Press, 1935.

Goodwin, Grenville. *Myths and Tales of the White Mountain Apache*. New York: American Folklore Society, 1939. Reprinted by the University of Arizona Press, 1994.

Malotki, Ekkehart, and Michael Lomatuway'ma. *Stories of Maasaw, a Hopi God*. Lincoln and London: University of Nebraska Press, 1987.

Matthews, Washington. *The Mountain Chant: A Navajo Ceremony*. Washington, D.C.: Smithsonian Institution, Bureau of American Ethnology, 5th Annual Report, 1887. Reprinted by the University of Utah Press, 1997.

———. *Navaho Legends*. Boston: Houghton Mifflin, 1897. Reprinted by the University of Utah Press, 1994.

———. *The Night Chant: A Navajo Ceremony*. New York: Knickerbocker Press, 1902. Reprinted by the University of Utah Press, 1995.

O'Brien, Aileen. *The Dîné: Origin Myths of the Navaho Indians*. Washington, D.C.: Smithsonian Institution, Bureau of American Ethnology, Bulletin 163, 1956. Reprinted as *Navaho Indian Myths* by Dover Publications, 1993.

Opler, Morris Edward. *Myths and Tales of the Chiricahua Apache Indians*. New York: American Folklore Society, 1942. Reprinted by the University of Nebraska Press, 1994.

———. *Myths and Tales of the Jicarilla Apache Indians*. New York: American Folklore Society, 1938. Reprinted by the University of Nebraska Press, 1994.

Parsons, Elsie Clews. *Pueblo Indian Religion*. Chicago: University of Chicago Press, 1939. Reprinted by the University of Nebraska Press, 1996.

———. *Tewa Tales*. New York: American Folklore Society, 1926. Reprinted by the University of Arizona Press, 1994.

Russell, Frank. *The Pima Indians*. Washington, D.C.: Smithsonian Institution, Bureau of American Ethnology, 26th Annual Report, 1908.

Tyler, Hamilton A. *Pueblo Gods and Myths*. Norman and London: University of Oklahoma Press, 1964.

Waters, Frank. *Book of the Hopi*. New York: Viking Press, 1963.

CALIFORNIA

Curtin, Jeremiah. *Creation Myths of Primitive America*. Boston: Little, Brown and Company, 1898.

———. *Myths of the Modocs*. Boston: Little, Brown and Company, 1912.

Dixon, Roland B. *Maidu Texts*. Publications of the American Ethnological Society, vol. 4. Leyden: E. J. Brill, 1912.

DuBois, Cora. *Wintu Ethnography*. University of California Publications in American Archaeology and Ethnology, vol. 36. Berkeley: University of California Press, 1935.

Gamble, Geoffrey. *Yokuts Texts*. Berlin and New York: Mouton de Gruyter, 1994.

Gifford, Edward W., and Gwendoline Harris Block. *Californian Indian Nights*. Glendale, Calif.: Arthur H. Clark Company, 1930. Reprinted by the University of Nebraska Press, 1990.

Goddard, Pliny Earle. *Hupa Texts*. University of California Publications in American Archaeology and Ethnology, vol. 1. Berkeley: University California Press, 1903–1904.

Kroeber, A. L. *Handbook of the Indians of California*. Washington, D.C.: Smithsonian Institution, Bureau of American Ethnography, Bulletin 78, 1925. Reprinted by Dover Books, 1976.

———. *Yurok Myths*. Berkeley, Los Angeles, London: University of California Press, 1976.

Merriam, C. Hart. *An-nik-a-del: The History of the Universe as Told by the Modés-se Indians of California*. Boston: The Stratford Co., 1928. Reprinted as *Annikadel* by the University of Arizona Press, 1928.

———. *The Dawn of the World: Myths and Weird Tales Told by the Mewan Indians of California*. Cleveland: Arthur H. Clark Company, 1910. Reprinted as *The Dawn of the World: Myths and Tales of the Miwok Indians of California* by the University of Nebraska Press, 1993.

Shipley, William. *The Maidu Indian Myths and Stories of Hanc'Ibyjim*. Berkeley, Calif.: Heyday Books, 1991.

THE GREAT BASIN AND PLATEAU

Boas, Franz. *Kutenai Tales*. Washington, D.C.: Smithsonian Institution, Bureau of American Ethnology, Bulletin 59, 1918.

Hines, Donald M. *The Forgotten Tribes: Oral Tales of the Teninos and Adjacent Mid-Columbia River Indian Nations*. Issaquah, Wash.: Great Eagle Publishing, Inc., 1991.

Hittman, Michael. *Wovoka and the Ghost Dance*. Edited by Don Lynch. Lincoln and London: University of Nebraska Press, 1997.

Sapir, Edward, and Jeremiah Curtin. *Wishram Texts, Together with Wasco Tales and Myths*. Leyden: E. J. Brill for the American Ethnological Society, 1909.

Smith, Anne M. *Ute Tales*. Salt Lake City: University of Utah Press, 1992.

Teit, James A., Marian K. Gould, Livingston Farrand, and Herbert J. Spinden. *Folk-Tales of Salishan and Sahaptin Tribes*. Edited by Franz Boas. Lancaster, Penn.: American Folklore Society, 1917.

Trafzer, Clifford E. *Grandmother, Grandfather, and Old Wolf: Tamánwit Ku Súkat and Traditional Native American Narratives from the Columbia Plateau*. East Lansing: Michigan State University Press, 1998.

Walker, Deward E., Jr. *Myths of Idaho Indians*. Moscow: University of Idaho Press, 1980.

———. and Daniel N. Matthews. *Nez Perce Coyote Tales: The Myth Cycle*. Norman: University of Oklahoma Press, 1998.

THE NORTHWEST

Barbeau, Marius. *Haida Myths*. Ottawa: National Museum of Canada. 1953.

Boas, Franz. *Bella Bella Tales*. New York: G. E. Stechert and Co., 1932.

———. *Tsimshian Mythology*. Washington, D.C.: Smithsonian Institution, Bureau of American Ethnology, 31st Annual Report, 1916.

Curtis, Natalie. *The Indians' Book*. New York: Harper and Brothers, 1923. Reprinted by Dover Publications, 1968.

Dauenhauer, Nora Marks, and Richard Dauenhauer. *Haa Shuká, Our Ancestors: Tlingit Oral Narratives*. Seattle and London: University of Washington Press, and Juneau: Sealaska Heritage Foundation, 1987.

Garfield, Viola E., Paul S. Wingert, and Marius Barbeau. *The Tsimshian: Their Arts and Music*. New York: J. J. Augustin, 1953.

McIlwraith, T. F. *The Bella Coola Indians* (2 vols.). Toronto: University of Toronto Press, 1948.

Maud, Ralph. *A Guide to B.C. Indian Myth and Legend*. Vancouver: Talonbooks, 1982.

Sapir, Edward A., and Morris Swadesh. *Nootka Texts*. Philadelphia: Linguistic Society of America, 1939.

Swanton, John R. *Haida Texts and Myths*. Washington, D.C.: Smithsonian Institution, Bureau of American Ethnology, Bulletin 29, 1905.

———. *Tlingit Myths and Texts*. Washington, D.C.: Smithsonian Institution, Bureau of American Ethnology, Bulletin 39, 1909.

THE ARCTIC

Bierhorst, John. *The Dancing Fox: Arctic Folktales*. New York: William Morrow, 1997.

Hall, Edwin S. *The Eskimo Storyteller: Folktales from Noatak, Alaska*. Knoxville: University of Tennessee Press, 1975.

Lantis, Margaret. "The Mythology of Kodiak Island." *Journal of American Folklore*, vol. 51, 1938.

Lowenstein, Tom. *Ancient Land: Sacred Whale*. New York: Farrar, Straus and Giroux, 1993.

Nelson, Edward William. *The Eskimo About Bering Strait*. Washington, D.C.: Smithsonian Institution, Bureau of American Ethnology, 18th Annual Report, 1899. Reprinted by Smithsonian Institution Press, 1983.

Norman, Howard. *Northern Tales: Traditional Stories of Eskimo and Indian Peoples*. New York: Pantheon, 1990.

Oman, Lela Kiana. *The Epic of Qayak: The Longest Story Ever Told by My People*. Ottawa: Carleton University Press, and Seattle: University of Washington Press, 1995.

Rasmussen, Knud. *Across Arctic America*. New York: Putnam, 1927. Reprinted by Greenwood Press, 1969.

———. *Eagle's Gift: Alaska Eskimo Tales*. Garden City, N.Y.: Doubleday, Doran & Company, 1932.

———. *Eskimo Folk-Tales*. London and Copenhagen: Gyldendal, 1921.

———. *Intellectual Culture of the Iglulik Eskimos*. Copenhagen: Gyldendal, 1930.

———. *The Nestilik Eskimos: Social Life and Spiritual Culture*. Copenhagen: Gyldendal, 1931.

Rink, Hinrich. *Tales and Traditions of the Eskimo*. Edinburgh and London: William Blackwood and Sons, 1875. Reprinted by Dover Publications, 1997.

ACKNOWLEDGMENTS

This book could never have been written without the efforts of hundreds of scholars who have worked tirelessly to record the myths of Native Americans. In turn, the work of those scholars would have been impossible without the collaboration of the native storytellers and tradition-bearers who have so generously shared their knowledge with us. I am grateful and indebted to them all.

The bibliography lists the books I have relied on most directly; I have consulted many others that there was no room to list. A much fuller bibliography can be found in Sam D. Gill and Irene F. Sullivan's *Dictionary of Native American Mythology*, a work I have found invaluable.

For permission to reproduce photographs, grateful acknowledgment is made to the following institutions, with particular thanks to Paula Richardson Fleming at the Smithsonian Institution, Jeremy Smith at the Guildhall Library, and Geremy Butler for special photography:

Guildhall Library, Corporation of London: endpapers, half-title page, dedication, facing contents, 3, 4, 12, 16, 19, 46, 50, 55, 65, 69, 73, 76, 80, 83, 84, 92, 94, 98, 101, 102, 104, 110, 114, 119, 123, 127, 128, 130, 133; **Library of Congress:** facing page 1 (58914), 11 (101185), 27 (101333), 45 (100432), 49 (101188), 66 (103650), 117 (10926), 120 (101170), 134 (101282); **National Anthropological Archives, Smithsonian Institution:** title page (1982-C), 7 (56,814), 8 (4130-A), 22 (476-A-20), 24 (1044-B), 28 (616-W-1), 31 (1000-B), 32 (1008), 37 (1102-B-14), 40 (44,353-C), 52 (56,258), 56 (77-13,305), 59 (1285), 62 (1821-A-2), 71 (76-6299), 75 (41,106-B), 78 (76-15807), 87 (56,770), 107 (55,298), 108 (1659-C), 113 (38,582-D); **Phoebe Apperson Hearst Museum of Anthropology, and the Regents of the University of California at Berkeley:** 90 (15-3329).

INDEX

Above Old Man, 81
Achomawi, 2, 81, 82
acorns, 79, 86, 91
Alabama, 29, 39–42
Algonquin, 14, 17, 23
altar, 47, 52; *see also* buffalo skull
Ancient One, 14–15
animal-people, 5, 35, 85–91, 99–100, 111–16, 117, 122, 124, 131–35; *see also* First People, raw people, *woge*
Ani-Tsaguhi, 35–38
Antelope Society, 5
Apache, 5, 67, 72, 74–75
Arapaho, 56–57, 106
Arctic, 125–35, 140
Arikara, 10, 48, 54
Athapaskan, 17
Atotarho, 21
Atseemath, *see* transformers
Awonawilona, 5, 6

Bacon Rind, 9
ball game, 24–26, 57; *see also* Throwing the Ball
basket dice game, 51–53
basketry, 85, 91
bear, 18, 35–38, 105, 111, 122, 124, 126
Bear Clan, 9
Bear Mother, 124
beaver, 3, 18, 58, 99–100, 102, 111, 112, 116
Beaver's Grandchild, 29
Bella Bella, 124
Bella Coola, 11, 111, 121
Bierhorst, John, 3
Big Black Meteoric Star, 52–53
Big Foot, 106
Big Head Dance, 79
Black Elk, 9, 13, 44, 57
Blackfoot, 43, 53–54
blasphemy, 131
Blowsnake, Jasper, 13
Boas, Franz, 117
Born for Water, 63, 64; *see also* Child of the Water
Breath Maker, 41
Bright Cloud Woman, 121
Brown, Joseph Epes, 9
Brush Dance, 83
buffalo, 43, 45, 47–48, 49–51, 55, 56, 59
Buffalo Dance, 10, 44, 46–47, 51; *see also* Okeepa
buffalo skull, 44, 47, 48; *see also* altar
Buffalo Woman, 49–51, 54; *see also* White Buffalo Maiden
Bull Child, 6
butterfly, 68
buzzard, 30, 68–72

Caddo, 35
California, 2, 79–93, 139
canoe, 20, 26, 39–42, 81, 84; *see also* kayak
cardinal directions, 10, 41, 47, 54, 74
caribou, *see* reindeer
Case, 121
Catlin, George, 44
Cayuga, 14, 21
center of the world, 45, 82; *see also* cardinal directions
ceremonies, *see* rituals
Changing Woman, 10, 64
chantways, 64–68
Chase, A. W., 86
Chased by Bears, 44
Cherokee, 25, 29–40
Cheyenne, 43, 51, 58
Chickasaw, 29
Chief Big Kittle, 18
Chief Coudawhot, 116
Chief Elk, 6
Chief Joseph, 95–96
Child of the Water, 74, 75; *see also* Born for Water
Chilkat, 116
Chipewyan, 17
Chippewa, *see* Ojibwe
Choctaw, 29, 36
Christianity, 27–28; *see also* Jesus Christ
Chungichnish, 82
circle, 11, 44
clouds, 52, 63, 73, 81, 118
clowns, 74
Coast Salish, 97–99
Coeur d'Alene, 97, 100
Cold, *see* Cold Weather Brothers
Cold Weather Brothers, 100–1
Columbia River Indians, 100
Columbus, Christopher, 28
cooked people 5, *see* Real People
condor, 81
Copper Woman, 17
corn, 13, 16, 17, 30, 36, 41, 48, 54, 56

Corn ceremony, 54
Corn Mother, 48, 45, 54, 61; *see also* Iatiku, Old Woman Who Never Dies
Corn Woman, *see* Corn Mother
Cottontail, 97
Cowichan, 118
Coyote, 11, 36, 46, 69–70, 75–77, 81, 82–84, 85, 91, 95, 96, 97, 102–5; *see also* trickster
crawfish, 29
creation, 1, 4–5, 10, 14–17, 18, 29–30, 43, 45–46, 47, 56, 58, 61–63, 64, 68–72, 72–74, 79, 81, 82, 93, 96, 109, 116, 125, 126; *see also* dual creators, end of the world
creation time, 5, 11, 53, 79–82, 85–91, 95, 107, 111, 116, 118, 124
creators, *see* Above Old Man, Ancient One, Awonawilona, Coyote, dual creators, Earth Doctor, Earthmaker, Earth Mother, Empty, First Creator, Fish Eater, Flint, God, Glooscap, Grandfather, Great Chief Above, Great Mystery, Great Spirit, Hawk, Lone Man, Lord of the Sky, Malsum, Man Never Known on Earth, Mink, Na'pi, Old Man, Old One, Olelbis, Ones Who Hold Our Roads, Pulekukwerek, Raven, Silver Fox, Sky Holder, Supreme God, sun, Taiowa, Thinking Woman, Tirawa, Vacant, Wakan Tanka, Walks All Over the Sky, Wohpekumeu, Wolf, World's Heart
Cree, 18
Creek, 11, 25, 29, 30, 38, 39
crow, 74, 106; *see also* raven
Crow, 13, 53
Crow Dog, Leonard, 57
Crown Dancers, *see* Gan Dancers
Crying for a Vision, 57; *see also* vision, vision quest
crystal, 33
culture hero, 10, 79
Curtis, Edward S., 3, 5, 10, 13, 17, 18, 47, 48, 51, 51, 54, 64, 69, 72, 77, 81, 83, 85, 93, 95, 99, 100, 103, 105, 111, 115, 118, 122, 127, 129, 131, 132

Dakota, *see* Sioux
dancing, 11, 27, 28, 33, 34, 41, 44, 45–48, 51, 52–53, 64, 72, 74, 77, 79, 81, 83, 105–6, 112–16, 118, 122, 132–35

Dances, *see* Big Head Dance, Brush Dance, Buffalo Dance, Deerskin Dance, Dream Dance, Eagle Dance, Gan Dancers, Ghost Dance, Green Corn Dance, Jumping Dance, Medicine Dance, Okeepa, Rain Dance, Round Dance, Snake Dance, Sun Dance, Weather Dancers, Winter Dances, Wolf Dance, Woman's Dance
Darkening Land, *see* dead, land of the
Daylight Boy, 67
Daylight Girl, 67
Daughter of the Sun, 30–35, 39
death, 31, 33–35, 42, 53–54, 61, 81, 82, 83–84, 91, 93, 96, 105, 106, 109, 117
dead, land of the, 33, 35, 83, 106, 109
deer, 81, 89–91
Deerskin Dance, 81
Deganawida, 18–21, 22
DeMallie, Raymond J., 57
Devil, 28
Digueño, 93
dog, 30, 58, 81, 89–91, 129, 131
Dorsey, George A., 47
Draper, 121
Dream Dance, 27, 28
Dreamer religion, 100
dreaming, 5, 27
drumming, 28, 34, 47, 132
dual creators, 10, 15–17, 18, 46, 62–63, 79, 81, 82, 91, 96–97
duck, 56
Dusty Dress, 99

eagle, 1, 22, 77, 131–35
Eagle Dance, 77
eagle feathers, 5, 47, 106
Eagle Society, 77
earth, 1, 5, 9, 14–17, 18, 69, 82, 122
earth diver, 10, 15, 29, 46, 56–57
Earth Daughter, 74
Earth Doctor, 68–72
Earthmaker, 82–84, 91
Earth Mother, 1, 5, 122; *see also* First Mother, Grandmother Earth, Old Woman
earthquake, 121
Eatgentci, 17
Elder Brother, 69–72
Eleusis, Mysteries of, 13
emergence, myth of the, 29, 44–45, 61, 75
Empty, 82
end of the world, 42, 58, 59, 61, 72, 93, 106
Erdoes, Richard, 4
ermine, 122
Evening Star, 52–53, 58, 59

Falling Star, 51–53
False Faces, 21, 28
fasting, 13, 27
fertility, 9
fire, 30, 41, 43, 85, 99, 122, 126

fire, theft of, 85–91, 99–100
Fire People, 99
Fire Thunder, Edgar, 6
First Creator, 10, 46
first–fruits festival, 11, 30, 41
First Man, 64; *see also* human beings, creation of
First Mother, 17–18; *see also* Earth Mother, Old Woman
First People, 5, 79, 85–91, 99–100, 111–16, 117, 122, 124, 131–35; *see also* animal–people, *woge*
First Woman, 64
fish, 23–24, 38, 74–75, 79, 81, 95, 96, 102–104, 111, 118, 121, 122; *see also* salmon
Fish Eater, 96
fishing, 95, 102–4, 111, 118, 127
Five Civilized Tribes, 29
Fletcher, Alice, 6
Flint, 16–17, 18, 28
flood, 10, 15, 26, 34, 46, 47, 56, 59, 74, 81, 85, 93
Foolish One, 47
Fools Crow, Frank, 58
Fort Laramie Peace Talks, 57
Four Bears, 57
fox, 135
Freddy, Mrs., 91
frog, 93, 105, 112, 115, 115,
Frog Brothers, 105
fulmar, 129

gambling, 48, 49, 51, 53
games, 24–26, 48, 49, 51–53
Gan Dancers, 74
Gardner, Alexander, 57
Ghost Country, *see* dead, land of the
Ghost Dance, 105–9
Gichi Manitou, 27
Gill, Sam D., 3
Girl Without Parents, 73–74
giveaway feast, *see* potlatch
Gives Everything, 41
Glooscap, 18
goat, 122
God, 109
Goddard, Pliny Earle, 91
Good Seat, 43
Grandfather, 56
Grandmother Earth, 9; *see also* Earth Mother, First Mother, Old Woman
Great Basin and Plateau, 95–109, 139
Great Chief Above, 96
Great Green Lizard, 86
Great Mystery, 6–7, 27, 43–44
Great Spirit, 10, 21, 23, 27, 28, 43, 46, 95
Great Sun, 30
Great White Bear, 26
Greece, 6, 13
Green Corn Dance, 41
Grinnell, George Bird, 13
grizzly bear, 105

hactcin, 67

Haida, 116
Handsome Lake, 23
Happiness Girl, 64
harvest festival, *see* first-fruits festival
Havasupai, 72
Hawenniyo, 21, 28
Hawk, 96
Hayicanako, *see* Old Woman Underneath Us
healing, 18, 23, 77
Heat, *see* Warm Weather Brothers
Herald of Dawn, 93
hero twins, 63; *see also* Little War Gods
Heyn, Herman, 1
Hiawatha, 18–21
Hidatsa, 54
hiding the stone, 53
Hittman, Michael, 109
Holy People, 67
hoop-and-pole game, 49
Hopi, 2, 4, 5, 11, 61, 63, 66
horned serpent, 27, 32–33, 39; *see also* Uktena
House God, 69
House of Myths, 111
human beings, creation of, 17, 47, 51, 53, 54, 58, 63, 68, 72, 74, 81, 96, 125, 126; *see also* Real People
hummingbird, 35
hunting, 5, 18, 37, 49, 54, 66, 74, 95, 96, 100, 104, 111, 124, 128–29, 131–32
Hupa, 81, 91

Iatiku, 61–63; *see also* Corn Mother
igloo, 126
Iglulik, 131
Iktomi, 43
inkoze, 17
initiation rites, 3, 5, 10, 82
Inuit, 125–35
inua, 126
Inupiat, *see* Inuit
Inyan, 43
Iroquois, 5, 14, 21
Istet Woiche, 2
Iya, 43

jackrabbit, 89
Jackson, William Henry, 58
Jenks, A. E., 23
Jesus Christ, 28
jimsonweed, *see* toloache
Juaneño, 81–82
Jumping Dance, 81

Kaa-Claa, 121
kachina, 2, 63, 66
Kalispel, 99
Kánikala, *see* transformers
Karok, 79
Kathlamet, 124
Kaviagamute, 135
kayak, 126, 128, 130
Keeping of the Soul, 57

Keres, 61–63, 68
Killer of Enemies, 74, 75; *see also* Monster Slayer
killer whale, 111
Kixunai, *see* First People
Koskimo,115
Kuksu cult, 79
Kwakiutl, 111, 112–16, 117, 124

lacrosse, *see* ball game
La Flesche, Francis, 6, 9
Lake Miwok Indians, *see* Miwok
Lakota, 6, 9, 43, 44, 57, 58, 106; *see also* Sioux
Last Horse, 1
laws, 18–21, 22, 53, 56, 75, 79, 81, 82, 103, 107, 117
lightning, 52, 88, 99
Lightning Maker, 73
Lillooet, 96
Linde, Carl Gustav, 26
Little People, 31–33
Little War Gods 74; *see also* hero twins
Little Wound, 6
lizard, 91
Lomen Brothers, 135
Lone Man, 10, 46
longhouse, 14, 21, 23
Longhouse Religon, 23
Long Life Boy, 64
loon, 18, 85
Loon Woman, 85
Lord of the Sky, 116
Lowenstein, Tom,128
Luckie, Kate, 93
Luiseño, 81–82
lullabies, 38
lynx, 135

Madesiwi, 2
magical power, 5, 17, 27
magpie, 89
Mahtantu, 18
Maidu, 82, 85, 91
Mails, Thomas E., 58
Maker, 93
Making of Relatives, 57
Malsum, 18
Man Careful of His Horses, 57
Man Never Known on Earth, 54–46
Mandan, 10, 11, 44–47
manitou, 18, 27
Maricopa, 1
masks, 63, 64, 67, 69, 74, 115, 116, 118, 127, 131
Maskwa, 18
Master of Life, 27
McCoy, Tim, 109
McWhorter, Lucullus, 102, 105
medicine, 13
Medicine Bull, Mrs., 58
medicine bundle, 3, 23, 41, 48, 49, 50, 52, 54, 57, 64
Medicine Dance, 10, 27, 28
medicine man, 6, 33, 35, 44, 48, 52, 57; *see also* shaman

Mem Loimis, 82
Menapus, 28; *see also* Winabojo
Meninock, George, 104, 105
Menomini, 17, 23, 24, 26–27, 28
Merriam, C. Hart, 2, 79
messiah, 109
Midewiwin, 23
Milky Way, 30
Miller, Fred E., 53
mink, 18, 96, 122, 124
Miwok, 85
Mohawk, 14, 18–21
Monster Slayer, 63; *see also* Killer of Enemies
moon, 5, 13, 31, 39, 48, 49, 52–53, 58, 59, 63, 67, 69, 93, 97, 106, 129
Mooney, James, 25, 29, 33, 37, 63, 105, 106
Moonlight–Giving Mother, 5
Moon Man, 129
moose, 18
Morning Star, 58, 59
mosquito, 86–88
Mother Night Men, 10
Mountainway, 66–68
Mount Grant, 109
mouse, 89–91, 113–15
Mouth at Each End, 117
mudhen, 46
Murie, James R., 47, 48
Muskogee, 29
muskrat, 15, 18

Nakoaktok, 111
Nakota, *see* Sioux
Na'pi, 53–54; *see also* Old Man
Natchez, 30
Nautsiti, 63
Navajo, 11, 13, 61, 63–68, 69
Nelson, Edward William, 125
Netsilik, 129–31
Nez Perce, 95–96, 99–100, 105
Night, 10
nighthawk, 89
Nightway, 13, 64, 67
Nisenan, 86
Noatak, 135
Nootka, 122, 124
North, Major Frank, 13
Northeast, 14–28, 43, 136
North Star, 58
Northwest, 11, 111–24, 140
Nowell, Charles James, 112
Nuhlimkilaka, 115
núnhlim ceremony, 115

Ojibwe, 23, 26, 27, 28, 43
Okanagon, 96
Okeepa, 10, 11, 44, 46–47
O-ke-hée-de, 47
Old Man, 53–54, 103; *see also* Na'pi
Old One, 96
Old Woman, 14–17, 18, 103
Old Woman Underneath Us, 121
Old Woman Who Never Dies, 54; *see also* Corn Mother

Olelbis, 82
Omaha, 6
Oman, Lela Kiana, 129
Oneida, 14, 21
Ones Who Hold Our Roads, 5
One Who Lives Above, 73–74
Onondaga, 14, 18, 21
orenda, 5, 17
Orpheus, 35
Ortiz, Alfonso, 4
Osage, 9
owl, 66–67, 109
Owl Child, 102

Packs Wolf, 47
Paiute, 96, 97, 105–109
Paiyatemu, 2
Papago, 61, 68, 72
Parks, Douglas R., 57
Passamaquoddy, 18, 26
Pawnee, 13, 47–53, 58, 59
Penobscot, 17
Piegan, 3, 6
Pikavahairak, *see* creation time
Pima, 61, 68–72
Pine Ridge Reservation, 6, 57
Plains, 6–11, 13, 43–60, 95, 106, 137
Plateau, *see* Great Basin and Plateau
Pollen Girl, 74
Pomo, 79
Ponca, 44
Pond, Percy, 116
potlatch, 111, 112, 118, 121
Powamu Ceremony, 63
prayers, 11, 43, 64, 66–67, 99
Preparing for Womanhood, 57
pueblo, 61, 74
Pulekukwerek, 79
Purification Day, *see* end of the world

Qayak, 129

rabbit, 23, 28, 35, 93, 97
raccoon, 81
Radin, Paul, 13
rain, 5, 69, 72, 74
rainbow, 67
Rain Dance, 72
Rainmaker, 109
Rasmussen, Knud, 129, 131
raven, 111–21, 124, 125–29
raw people, 5
Real People, 79, 105
Reared Within the Mountain, 66–67
redbird, 34
Red Cloud, 57
reindeer, 126, 135
rites, *see* initiation rites, rituals
rituals, 1, 3, 5, 9, 10, 11, 13, 28, 30, 41, 44, 46–47, 48, 54, 57, 58, 61, 63, 64, 67, 77, 79, 81, 82, 103, 111, 112, 115, 116, 119, 121, 131; *see also* dances
Roaming Chief, 47, 59
rock, 43, 95
Rome, 6, 43

Round Dance, 106
Russell, Frank, 68

sacred pipe, 9, 21, 46, 47, 48, 54, 56, 57, 58
Sagluag, 131
Salish, 117; *see also* Coast Salish
salmon, 79, 81, 95, 96, 102–4, 111, 118, 121, 122
sand paintings, 64, 67
Sanpoil, 103
Schwemberger, Simeon, 67
sea beasts, mother of the, *see* Sedna
seal, 126, 129, 130
Sea Woman, *see* Sedna
Sedna, 129–31
self–torture, 44
Seminole, 25, 29, 41
Seneca, 14–17, 18, 23, 28
Sequoyah, 33
Seventh Cavalry, 106
shaman, 83, 93, 131
Shawnee, 23
sheep,126
Shoshone, 97
Silver Fox, 81
Sioux, 1, 6, 9, 13, 43, 44, 57–58, 106; *see also* Dakota, Lakota, Nakota
Skan, 57
Skate, 79
Skinner, Alanson, 28
skunk, 89, 90
sky, 69, 82
Sky Boy, 74
Sky Father, 1, 5; *see also* creators
Sky Holder, 16–17, 18, 23, 27, 28
sky world, 14, 17, 26, 39–42, 85–8, 97–99, 116, 118
slavery, 111
Slayer of the Alien Gods, *see* Monster Slayer
Small Boy, 73
smallpox, 44
Smohalla, 100
snake, 5, 31–33, 35, 38, 89, 90; *see also* horned serpent
Snake Dance, 5
snipe, 85
songs, 11, 33, 38, 52, 54, 64, 67–68, 106, 111, 113, 115, 122, 132–35
song festival, 133–35
Southeast, 11, 25, 29–42, 43, 137
South Star, 59
Southwest, 1, 2–5, 11, 13, 61–77, 138
spider, 63, 68
Spider Man, 43
Spider Woman, 63
spirit world, *see* dead, land of the
spirits, 5, 11, 13, 18, 54, 66, 67, 74, 79, 81, 93, 106, 115, 125, 131
Spokane, 100
sports, *see* games
Spotted Eagle, 6
Starisu, 47
Star Husband, 97–99

stars, 26, 30, 39, 51–53, 58, 59, 82, 93, 97–99, 116, 118
storytelling, 1, 5, 11, 91, 111, 112, 129, 131
Sullivan, Irene F., 3
Supreme God, 28
sun, 2, 5, 9, 17, 26, 30–35, 43, 44, 58, 63, 64, 69–71, 73, 74, 97, 106, 109, 105, 118–21, 126
Sun Chief, 58
Sun Dance, 6, 30, 44, 57, 58; *see also* Okeepa
Sun Father, 5
Sun God, *see* sun
swallow, 103
Swan, James G., 112
sweat lodge, 9, 57, 66, 74, 85
Swimmer, 30, 33
Sword, George, 6

Taiowa, 2, 4–5
Talking God, 64, 66–67, 69
Tate, Henry W., 117
tattoos, 9
Tecumseh, 23
Tenskatawa, 23
Teriak, 131–135
Tewa, 77
Thinking Woman, 61–63, 68; *see also* Spider Woman
Thin Leather, 68
Throwing the Ball, 57; *see also* ball game
thunder, 27, 39, 52, 85–91
thunderbird, 26, 27
Tikigaq, 128
Tirawa, 47, 48, 49, 53, 58
Tlingit, 121
tobacco, 3, 15, 16, 28, 35, 44, 67
toloache, 82
totem pole, 111, 112–16, 117, 124
Trafzer, Clifford E., 102
transformers, 97, 116–17, 124, 129
trickster, 10, 18, 35, 36, 43, 75–77, 79, 116, 121, 124
Tsagiglálal, 95
Tsimshian, 116, 117–21
Tu-chai-pai, *see* Maker
Tunica, 30
turtle, 15, 45, 47, 56, 57, 91
Turtle Island, 14
Tuscarora, 14
Two Whistles, 13
Tyon, Thomas, 57

Uktena, 32–33, 39; *see also* horned serpent
Unalit, 125
underworld, 15, 25, 26, 33, 39, 61, 75
unknown god, the, 43
Ute, 66–67

Vacant, 82
vision, 5, 13, 44, 57; *see also* Crying for a Vision
vision quest, 5

wakan, 6, 9, 57
Wakan Tanka, 6, 9, 43, 57
Wakashan, 117
Wakiash, 112–16
Wakon'da, 6–7
Walker, J. R., 6, 43, 57
Walks All Over the Sky, 116
Wambli, 1
wampum, 20–21
Wampum Code, 22
Wander-Hawk, *see* Qayak
Warm Weather Brothers, 100–1
warriors, 1, 9
water beetle, 29
Waters, Frank, 4
Weather Dancers, 6
weaving, 63
Welsit Manatu, 18
Wesucechak, 18
whale, 111, 126–29
Whale House, 116
White Buffalo Maiden, 57–58
White Goose Girl, 85
White Painted Woman, 74, 75
White Shell Woman, 64, 74, 75
Wichita, 56
Wilson, Jack, *see* Wovoka
Winabojo, 23–26; *see also* Menapus
wind, 15, 27, 52, 74
Winnebago, 13
Winter, Lloyd, 116
Winter Dances, 11, 118
Wintu, 82, 85, 93
Wishram, 95, 102
Wiyot, 81
Wodziwob, 109
wolf, 18, 135
Wolf Dance, 122, 135
wolverine, 135
woge, 79–80; *see also* First People
Wohpe, *see* White Buffalo Maiden
Wohpekumeu, 79
wolf, 96, 109
Woman Cleanse the People, 51
Woman's Dance, 47
World's Heart, 2, 82
world tree, 14–15, 21, 22, 111
Wounded Knee, Battle of, 106
Wovoka, 100, 105–9
Wuwuchim, 3

Yakima, 96, 104, 105
Yei, *see* Holy People
Yeibichai, *see* Nightway, Talking God
Yellow Wolf, 105
Yimantuwingyai, 81
Yokuts, 85, 91
Young Bull, 59
Younger Brother, 70
Young, Tom, 91
Yuchi, 29, 30
Yup'ik, *see* Inuit
Yurok, 79–80

Zuñi, 2, 5, 61, 72